BLOODSHED AT THE BROKEN SPUR

When Gordon Dugdale is murdered, his father, the wealthy owner of the Broken Spur ranch in Arizona, threatens to take the law into his own hands. Now it is up to Jeremiah Meade of the Governor's office to find the real killer before there is a lynching. Someone is out to get the Dugdale family — but who and why? And can Meade discover who is responsible before the plot for revenge succeeds and all the Dugdales are dead?

STEVEN GRAY

BLOODSHED AT THE BROKEN SPUR

Complete and Unabridged

LINFORD
Leicester

First published in Great Britain in 2011 by
Robert Hale Limited
London

First Linford Edition
published 2012
by arrangement with
Robert Hale Limited
London

British Library CIP Data

Gray, Steven.
Bloodshed at the Broken Spur.- -
(Linford western library)
1. Western stories.
2. Large type books.
I. Title II. Series
823.9′14–dc23

ISBN 978–1–4448–1312–8

Published by
F. A. Thorpe (Publishing)
Anstey, Leicestershire

Set by Words & Graphics Ltd.
Anstey, Leicestershire
Printed and bound in Great Britain by
T. J. International Ltd., Padstow, Cornwall

This book is printed on acid-free paper

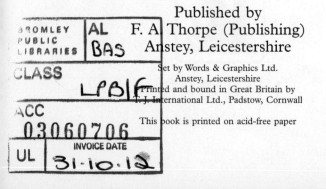

1

The air was filled with the sounds of shots and pleas for mercy that went unheard. With the screams of the wounded. Blood soaked into the dusty earth and coloured red the water of the nearby stream. The dead and dying lay along the edges of the road, under the trees and in the water.

Gus Dugdale woke up in a sweat. His heart was pounding. He hadn't suffered the nightmare for a long while now. And he couldn't understand why he continued to be haunted by what had happened so many years ago. It had occurred in the last days of the War Between the States and most of the time he never gave it a thought. And while others had come to call the incident The Atrocity he preferred to call it an act of war.

Carefully so as not to wake his wife,

he rolled out of bed. He crossed over to the window and pushed the curtain aside to peer out at the night, pressing his hot forehead against the glass.

If he was honest he had, on the whole, enjoyed the War. No, that wasn't right exactly. There had been little enjoyable about either the dirt or the mud of the endless marches or the boredom of camp when nothing seemed to happen for weeks on end of waiting. But the battles! All that fear and excitement! He'd felt alive then with every moment coloured by the fact that he could soon be dead.

And while The Atrocity couldn't be called a battle it had certainly been exciting. He didn't regret it, never had and never would, because at the time it had seemed right. Those who condemned him simply didn't understand.

'What's the matter?' His wife's sleepy voice came from the bed.

'Nothing, Celia. Go back to sleep. It's all right.'

So it was. For what did he have to

worry about or fear?

His life was all he had ever desired. He was married to his childhood sweetheart whom he still loved as much as ever, even after all these years together. And when the War was over she had followed him, without complaint, from their comfortable but dull home in Maine into an unknown future in the deserts of Arizona so he could fulfil his long-held dream of becoming a rancher.

Things had been difficult at first but he'd never once regretted his decision. Everything had turned out well. For what a ranch he now owned! The Broken Spur — the biggest and most successful spread in the area. Thousands of acres. Thousands of cattle. Good horseflesh. A large house with furniture and fittings shipped out from the best stores in the East. He and his family wore good clothes, ate good food, drank French wine.

And the future was secure. He had two grown up sons, who loved the cattle business as he did, and in whose good hands he could leave the ranch. A beautiful high-spirited daughter, who would eventually make a splendid marriage.

Maybe he'd had to do some terrible things in the past to get where he was today but it was a harsh land out here and in order to survive and succeed — and Dugdale had always been determined to do both — a person had to be ruthless.

These days he was a man of importance and wealth. A force to be reckoned with. Scared of no one and nothing. He could sit back, relax and enjoy his life, his family and his money.

The nightmare didn't mean anything.

He went back to bed believing there was nothing whatsoever to trouble him.

What could possibly go wrong in his life?

2

With a smirk Gordon Dugdale placed his five cards on the table: king of hearts, queen of spades, jack of clubs, ten of diamonds and nine of spades. A straight! Nothing could beat it!

'How's that for a winning hand, Mr Johnny Reb? Mine I believe?' Smirking again at the man across from him he started to reach for the pot of money.

'Not so fast, son,' the man drawled. He laid down his own cards. 'I happen to have four sevens and so that makes it mine.' Quickly he gathered up the pile of coins and notes.

Gordon's smirk changed to a snarl. How could this be happening to him? He was losing. At poker. Losing a great deal of money too. This was the third game in a row he'd lost, and all of them to this man, a stranger to Sycamore Corner. And who, to add considerable insult to injury, was from his voice and dress every inch a Southerner. Either he was a helluva lucky player or he was a better cheat than Gordon, because he certainly couldn't be more skilled. Even worse, Gordon was aware that the other two men at the table were relishing his discomfort.

'Damn Reb,' he muttered.

'You've been calling me that since we sat down to play,' the man said with a dangerous glint in his eyes that a more prudent person than Gordon would have taken notice of. 'I'm beginning to dislike it. As a matter of fact I'm beginning to dislike you too.'

Gordon slapped his hands down on the table and leant forward. 'Watch it, mister. My pa was a colonel in the Union Army and he and the men who work for him don't like Rebs any more'n I do.'

'War's been over a long time, son.'

'Not out on the Broken Spur it ain't,' one of the other men said with a grin that didn't make Gordon feel any better because he wasn't sure whose side was being taken. 'They take it real seriously out there.'

'And always will,' Gordon snapped. 'We know how to treat Rebs.'

If things were bad already they were made worse when, at that moment, the saloon's swing doors were pushed back and Ralph Addington came in. Gordon saw him and glared. Almost at once Ralph spotted Gordon too but instead of stopping and turning round, which, having no wish to be in the same vicinity as the rancher's son, he usually did and which would be the sensible thing to do now, he continued on up to the bar.

How dare he! Gordon scowled even harder.

Angie, one of the saloon's two prostitutes, came up behind him, draping an arm around his shoulders. Before she could speak he shrugged her off.

'Bring me another whiskey.'

'Don't you think you've had enough?'

'Get me one! Now dammit!'

'Angie.' Tony Vaughan beckoned to her from where he was busy serving drinks behind the bar. 'Angie, give Gordy his whiskey then go tell Christine there's likely to be trouble.' He nodded towards the other girl who was at the far side of the room talking to a cowboy and was unaware of the situation. 'Find yourselves a couple of guys and go upstairs.'

The young woman nodded. She'd seen Gordon in an ugly and unpredictable mood before. The young man could be pleasant enough, good company and generous mostly, but there were other times, and this was one of them, when it was best to avoid him.

Vaughan turned to Ralph. 'And you, I don't want no trouble, understand?'

'You won't get any from me,' the young man said with a shrug.

Nevertheless trouble came to Ralph.

After Gordon downed his whiskey in one swallow he decided he didn't want to play any more poker. By losing, especially to a Southerner, he was making himself a laughing stock. Best walk away now with what dignity he could muster and hope his fellow gamblers soon forgot his embarrassment. Besides, God only knew what his father would say when he found out how much money his son had gambled away in one evening. He couldn't afford to lose any more.

'Count me out,' he said. He gathered up what little remained in front of him and got unsteadily to his feet. 'And don't you forget,' he pointed a finger at the stranger and made one last face-saving threat, 'clear outta town or dammit I'll ride back here with some of Pa's men and make sure you wish you had.'

Satisfied with the warning he glanced around the saloon only to find that no one was taking any notice of him and that Angie had disappeared. Just when he needed her too. Was the whole world against him? Feeling very sorry for himself he half-sauntered, half-staggered over to the bar. He ended up close to

Ralph but whether by design or accident probably even Gordon himself couldn't have said.

He slammed his glass down on the bar. 'Fill it up,' he ordered, then swung round to sneer at Ralph. But the young man had deliberately turned his back on him. Rage filled Gordon's heart and his face reddened. No one snubbed a Dugdale. Not even the doctor who, because he'd studied at some fancy Eastern University, considered himself better than everyone else. Especially not the doctor.

'C'mon, Gordy,' Vaughan pleaded with him. 'Go somewhere and sleep it off. You'll only get yourself into a fix.'

Naturally Gordon took no notice. 'Hey, Ralph.'

At a signal from Vaughan one of the saloon's more sensible customers ran outside to fetch Marshal Cassidy. Most everyone else sensed trouble and stayed put. Vaughan just hoped the marshal would be easily found. Cassidy was young and inexperienced but he was

10

already proving a reasonably good lawman and he should be able to prevent Gordon Dugdale from doing anything he, and probably others too, would regret.

'Ralph!' Gordon repeated in a harsher tone and poked him in the shoulder. 'Goddammit look at me! Hey, Ralphie, you seen any more of Polly? How's she doing? She had the baby yet?'

At last Ralph looked round, his face twisting with fury. 'You bastard!'

Gordon grinned. 'Hell, I don't know what you're so annoyed about. You could've had her once I'd finished with her. And just because I didn't want her no more it didn't mean I no longer cared. I got Pa to pay her a deal of money when she decided to leave town.'

'Bastard!' Ralph said again. He threw his beer, glass and all, at Gordon.

It was the excuse the other needed. He flung himself at Ralph, one hand bunching into a fist that he used to punch the young doctor in the face. As

Ralph swayed back against the bar, Gordon hit him again, this time aiming for his stomach.

Realizing it was coming, Ralph managed to twist his body slightly, so the blow took him in the side. He grunted in pain. Then somehow he got his own punches in: one, two, three. The last almost knocked Gordon over.

'Stop it! You fools!'

Vaughan's yell was lost in the yells and shouts of the men crowded into the saloon. As soon as the fight started everyone stopped what they were doing and clustered round to witness it. Probably most of them hoped that just for once Gordon would get his come-uppance and be beaten. It was a forlorn hope. Few people ever beat Gus Dugdale or his elder son at anything.

And Gordon was much the stronger of the two. He'd grown up on a ranch, handling horses, cattle and the dangers of the desert. He was used to fighting and defending himself. Ralph wasn't. He was a doctor, who had always lived in a town and who, usually, turned the other cheek.

Gordon felled him, kicked him hard a couple of times, before dragging him up only to knock him down again with a blow to the side of his head.

'That's enough!' Vaughan cried out. 'He's had enough. Leave him be.'

Normally Gordon would have done just that. Strutted away the victor and taken Angie to bed to boast to her about how strong and manly he was. Not tonight. Tonight, with all that had gone on since he entered the saloon, his blood-lust was up. He wasn't about to see sense and walk away.

God only knew how far he would go when he was in a rage as bad as this. And Vaughan was just wondering if any of his customers would help him subdue the young man when, thank the lord, Cassidy came into the saloon.

The marshal quickly summed up the situation and pushed his way through the baying crowd, drawing his revolver as he did so. Even as Gordon was reaching for Ralph again, Cassidy came up behind him. He used his revolver to hit the rancher's son round the back of the head.

Gordon collapsed to the saloon floor without so much as a groan and lay there, out cold.

'Silly fool,' Vaughan muttered. 'Thanks, Sam, it was turning real nasty. Gordy's drunk as a skunk.'

'Ralph, you hurt?' Cassidy turned to the doctor.

Ralph sat up, rather uncertainly, his hand going to his jaw. 'I don't think so. Not bad anyway.'

'Well, go on home and rest up. Someone help him. And you two,' Cassidy indicated a couple of relatively sober townsmen, 'get this idiot down to the cells. The rest of you go on about your business. Show's over.' And he turned back to Vaughan to find out exactly what had happened.

3

It was very late the next morning when Gordon Dugdale finally stirred and opened his eyes. For a moment or two he couldn't figure out where he was until he realized he was lying on a hard bunk bed in a jail cell. He sat up and groaned. It was hardly the first time he'd woken up in the same place feeling the same way. His head throbbed and his stomach churned from all the whiskey he'd drunk the evening before, but this time there was something more — the back of his head thumped like hell. With shaky fingers he reached to touch it and felt a large lump. All of a sudden he remembered. He'd been buffaloed by that damn hick marshal.

Hearing movement, Cassidy left his desk and came to lounge against the bars of the cell. 'Awake then? At last.'

Gordon tried to get to his feet but

gave up when everything swayed around him, promptly collapsing back down. For a moment he put his head in his hands wondering if he was going to be sick, then when the feeling passed he looked up and scowled at the marshal.

'You hit me from behind, dammit. I'll have you for that,' he threatened. 'Pa won't like what you did to me.' He stopped, thinking he sounded like a spoilt child. Even worse, so did Cassidy if his grin was anything to go by.

'I shouldn't say anything to him if I were you because I doubt your pa will like the fact you were brawling in the saloon with someone half your size.'

Gordon almost said that Ralph had started it but decided that was even more childish. Besides the marshal was right. He could do little wrong in his father's eyes except when it might give the Broken Spur ranch a bad name.

'I had to stop you before you did something that'd get you into real trouble,' Cassidy went on. 'Won't you ever learn?'

'You going to charge me?' Apprehensively, one of Gordon's hands curled round the other.

'Not this time. But only because Ralph wasn't too badly hurt and Vaughan said that while you landed the first blow you had some provocation.'

Cassidy also thought Ralph should have left the saloon once he realized Gordon was in there. He might have known the bad blood between the two would spill over into a fight, in which he would come off worse. But when Cassidy had gone to see how Ralph was this morning he had said he was tired of turning the other cheek to Gordon's jeers and spite; and Cassidy supposed he didn't really blame Ralph for that.

Gordon breathed a sigh of relief that he was going to be let go; he had the feeling that if he was hauled up in court the judge would come down hard on him. His father might believe otherwise but Gordon knew the Dugdale family — or at least certain members of it

— wasn't all that popular in Sycamore Corner.

'Just be careful. I might not be so lenient in the future. Now you can have some coffee and then be on your way.' Cassidy paused before going on. 'Gordy, a word of warning, it might be best if you didn't come back to town for a while. And when you do, don't go bad mouthing Polly Murdock.' He pointed a finger at the young man. 'People round here ain't any too fond of the way you treated that girl. Me included. Understand?'

'Yeah, sure,' Gordon agreed with a sulky twist of his mouth, although it was obvious he didn't understand what all the fuss was about. He went to stand up again and this time made it to his feet. He reached for the bars, clinging to them. 'Where's that damn coffee?'

Cassidy sighed, thinking that Gordon Dugdale ought to learn some much needed humility. He'd be better liked then.

* ★ ★

A little while later, as Cassidy watched him go, Gordon made his way from the jailhouse to The Sycamore Stop. The street was busy with men, women and children. No one took much notice of him, except that he was sure a couple of men he recognized from the saloon sniggered, making him wish he felt well enough to challenge them, while some of the women pulled their children out of his path. They probably believed he was still suffering from a hangover rather than the ill treatment of their marshal.

The Sycamore Stop was almost empty when he went inside. He collapsed at a table in one corner feeling very sorry for himself. Without being asked Tony Vaughan brought him over a beer.

Naturally, Gordon didn't thank him. Instead he said, 'Where's that god-damned Southerner was here last night?'

'He's gone.'

'Thought he'd leave. Pity though, I'd've liked the chance to beat some respect into him.' Gordon grinned. He liked the idea that the Rebel had left town with his tail between his legs scared of the threats he had made. But secretly he was also pleased the Southerner had gone. His head ached too much for him to want to start another fight and he had the feeling that if the Rebel had been as good at fisticuffs as he was at playing cards he would have come off worst. 'Where's Angie?'

Sobering up, Gordon was nearly always ashamed of himself and on his best behaviour but today he was also nursing a headache and his grievances and wouldn't be good company for anyone, so Vaughan said, 'She's busy. You should go on home,' he added, wiping down the table. 'Your pa'll be wondering where you are.'

'I don't need you to babysit me.' Gordon ran a hand through his hair. He didn't really feel up to the long ride to the ranch but if he wasn't back in good time for the evening meal his mother would worry. Then he'd be in even more trouble with his father and he had the feeling he was going to be in quite enough trouble as it was.

But he didn't want Vaughan to realize he was frightened of anybody so he deliberately took his time over his beer and even ordered some food. Then with a moody look on his face he went to the livery stable at the far end of the town and collected his horse. The journey usually took about an hour but it was hot and Gordon didn't feel well so he took his time, pretending it was for the sake of his horse.

By the time he'd almost reached the ranch it was turning cooler in the hill country. He felt better. His head no longer ached and he was hungry. He was pleased when he neared the bottom of the brush-covered hill down which he was riding. The buildings making up the ranch headquarters would soon come into view.

That was when he heard a strange sound.

In surprise he pulled his horse to a halt. What was it? Was it made by an animal? He didn't think so. But it was enough to chill his blood. As he stared at the shadows along the base of the hill he thought he saw something moving, over there by a stand of rocks.

'Who is it?'

His heart thumping with fear, his hand went towards his revolver. He never had the chance to draw it from its holster.

Instead the noise again echoed around the rocks — no, definitely not an animal, he thought with a shiver — and at the same time without any more warning there was the crack of a rifle.

The bullet slammed into Gordon's chest with such force that it knocked him backwards out of the saddle. As he landed on the ground with a thump that kicked up a spiral of dust, his horse whinnied in fright and galloped away.

Helpless, Gordon lay where he'd fallen, hardly able to breathe. His chest was suddenly painful and he could see blood staining the front of his white shirt. He tried to raise a violently shaking hand towards the wound but his arm had no strength in it and flopped back down. In fact there didn't seem to be any strength left in his whole body.

He'd been shot!

Hell, this couldn't be happening to him.

It wasn't fair. It wasn't right.

The shadow he thought he'd seen earlier moved away from the rocks and started to walk towards him, revealing itself to be a figure. A figure that held a rifle, and as it stopped by him, that rifle was raised and pointed at Gordon's body.

'No, please don't.' Gordon's voice came out in a croak. 'Please.'

The killer took no notice but slowly, relishing what was happening and the young man's fear, began to squeeze the trigger. And there wasn't one damn thing that Gordon could do about it.

★ ★ ★

Afterwards the killer walked away, feeling no remorse at what had been done. Actually feeling nothing but satisfaction. What would that bastard Gus Dugdale do or think about this: the death, the killing, of his elder son? It would be even better when he came to learn exactly what was happening to him and his family. The reason why. But that was a long way off and in the meantime he could suffer in ignorance. And that would be good too.

4

'Ah, Mr Meade, there you are, come on in and sit down,' said the Governor of the Territory of Arizona, indicating a chair on the other side of his desk. 'Did you have a good journey to Fort Verde?'

'Yes, sir.' Jeremiah Meade had just got back from delivering important government papers to the commanding officer of the fort which was situated some thirty-five miles away from Prescott. As soon as he returned he'd received the summons to go to the governor's mansion and he wondered what the urgency was.

He knew that whatever the task was that the governor wanted him to undertake he wouldn't refuse it.

A little while ago he had been working as a marshal in a small town over near Tucson but, bored with the day-to-day running of the marshal's office, and, at thirty-one, feeling the need to do something different, be someone more important, he had applied for a position in the governor's office. He hadn't been on the man's staff for very long, was still the new boy, and while he didn't have political ambitions he was anxious to do well and make his mark about the place. Impress those he worked for and with, show them he wasn't just a town marshal. Move into a better office than the cubby-hole he had at the moment.

Six feet tall, he was lean, with dark-brown hair and brown eyes. These days around town he mostly wore store-bought clothes and carried his revolver in a holster under his jacket, although when undertaking trips such as that to Fort Verde he dressed as he had done as a marshal, which was more sensible and more comfortable.

The governor tapped the week-old newspaper on his desk, whose front page was filled with the murder of Gordon Dugdale. 'Although it happened while you were at Fort Verde did you get a chance to read about this killing?'

'Yes, sir.' The young man's shooting had been front page news since it took place.

'It's created quite a stir. The newspapers have used it as an excuse to demand again that some action must be taken and quickly to stop the lawlessness in Arizona.' The governor sighed. 'It's all very well for those who write such articles. They're safe behind desks. They don't know the reality of life out here.'

'I quite agree, sir.' Meade thought a comment was in order. He knew that law and order, or rather the lack of it, was the main problem the governor had to face and the main criticism too.

'I'd like you to go to Sycamore Corner and look into exactly what happened.' The man held up his hand before Meade could speak. 'I know you've only just got back from a long ride and I normally wouldn't ask it but there's no one else I can spare. And more particularly no one else here who has worn a badge and who knows a thing or two about the law and arresting those responsible for breaking it.'

Meade thought arresting Saturday night drunks and rustlers was completely different from identifying and arresting a murderer but he didn't say so. He couldn't say he was best pleased about being used as a lawman by the governor but he wasn't about to complain. He didn't want to risk getting sacked or gain the reputation of being difficult.

'I'm sure it'll prove that the culprit is a disgruntled employee or perhaps a cowboy who works for a rival rancher. Someone like that. But . . . did you hear anything about Gus Dugdale while you were a marshal?'

'I've heard the name, that's all.'

'Well, let me tell you he's both rich and extremely powerful. He was also well known in the past for getting his own way by fair means or foul.' The governor sighed. 'You know what it was like for some of those men who came out here after the War. There was little in the way of authority to stop them when they took the law into their own hands nor even anyone to mind that they did so. In fact to be fair, it was often the only way to get things done. There were stories of rustlers disappearing on Dugdale's land or being found strung up without benefit of trial.'

Meade frowned. 'Surely all that was several years ago now? Isn't Dugdale respectable these days?'

'Oh yes, on the surface at least. But, as you're probably aware, a lot of these old-timers, Dugdale included, imagine they still live in the days when their word was all that counted.'

Meade had met quite a few people like that. 'They throw their weight around and make enemies as a consequence.'

'Exactly.'

Which could have been the reason

for his son's murder.

'Oh, mostly they keep within the law, behave themselves, but then something happens and they believe they can behave in the same old way they always have. That it's still their word that counts. But things *are* different these days.'

'What's the real problem, sir?'

The governor leant back in his chair, steepling his hands under his chin. 'I'm very much afraid that if the killer isn't arrested and soon, Dugdale might decide to do something about it personally. And it would cause all sorts of complications if he has to be arrested for murder, even for that of someone who eventually proves to be a murderer himself. Even worse, supposing he kills the wrong man?' He grimaced, imagining the sensation that would cause and obviously feeling that his own position might be at risk because of it.

'And no one's been arrested yet?' Meade asked.

'No.'

'Can't the county sheriff help?'

'Normally, yes, I expect he could. He's a good man who wouldn't stand for any nonsense. Unfortunately, he's away investigating rumours of Apache trouble on the far side of Bisbee. It'll take him a while to wrap that up.'

'What about the town marshal?'

'Marshal Samuel Cassidy. I'm told he's capable enough and people seem to like him. But he's young, only twenty-two, and inexperienced, having been in the job just a few months. Before that he was working in his father's dry goods store. Neither has he got a deputy to help him at the moment.' The governor spread his hands. 'Besides, as you're only too well aware, he's only responsible for the town, the ranch is outside of his jurisdiction and I doubt if Dugdale would take any notice of him if he didn't want to.'

With his own experiences to go by, Meade doubted that as well. In truth the rancher might not take any notice of the county sheriff either. Nor of him even though he would be acting with the governor's authority.

'You really believe Dugdale would lynch whoever he considered guilty?'

'Oh yes,' the governor said grimly.

'Even if there was no proof?'

'If he believed he had found the guilty party that would be all that mattered to him. Remember, he's a man who whenever he found a rustler on his land, dealt with him without bothering about a judge or a trial. Now, having just lost his first-born son, he's angry, grieving and quite capable of acting irrationally. He might regret his actions in the future but by then it would be too late.'

'The circumstances do make a difference.' As did the man.

'So, Mr Meade, what do you say? Will you go to Sycamore Corner and look into this for me?'

'Of course, sir.'

'Good. I knew I could count on you. I'll get a telegram sent to tell Marshal

Cassidy you're on your way and that he must give you any help you require. And I'll write a letter for you to take with you telling everyone, including Dugdale, that you're following my orders.' The man ran a hand through his hair. 'I hope you don't have too much difficulty in identifying the real culprit and arresting him.'

So did Meade!

'Or with Dugdale!'

5

Meade arrived in Sycamore Corner in the middle of the afternoon when it was stiflingly hot. As the stagecoach trundled down the main street he saw that, although the stores were open for business, very few people were about. And as the stagecoach came to a halt in front of a building that combined the coach company's office and livery stable as well as a barn, only a couple of small boys and a dog could be bothered to watch its arrival.

When he stepped down onto the sidewalk he was covered with dust and felt hot and sweaty from the long journey. He reached up to take his bag from the driver. 'Where's the marshal's office?'

The man pointed back the way they'd come. 'Down yonder.'

It would be! Still the walk gave Meade the chance to look at his surroundings.

The town appeared to consist of just the one main road, with a couple of short streets, lined with houses of all shapes and sizes, leading off it. Near to this, the business end of town, he found a red light district consisting of a couple of saloons, a billiards hall and a building that had to be a brothel.

Further along was a church half-hidden behind some sycamore trees and next to it a one-room schoolhouse. And they were followed by a few shops: the dry goods store, which must have been where Marshal Cassidy had once worked, a gun shop, a butcher's and another general store. They didn't have anything fancy about them but the windows looked well stocked with quality goods. Finally, there was a newspaper office and another building devoted to real estate.

Beyond them he reached the marshal's office standing next to a bank, which was good planning on someone's behalf. With a tiny hotel and a café opposite.

On the whole Meade was quite impressed.

Although the town was situated in the desert it was nonetheless a pleasant place with some greenery and sycamores growing all around. The trees with their barks of white and brown meant the presence of fresh, sweet-tasting ground water. Yes, it was a good spot, although it would probably never amount to much more than it was now because it was unlikely the railroad would ever come this way.

The marshal's office was built of adobe and inside it was reasonably cool. It consisted of just one large room with the office at the front and two cells at the back.

Samuel Cassidy was there at his desk. He was tall with brown hair, cut short, and brown eyes. His skin was tanned as if he spent a good deal of time outdoors and he looked at ease with the gun he wore on his hip. The office was neat and clean, just like the place where Meade worked. And as he stood up to shake

Meade's hand he didn't seem overwhelmed by someone from the governor's office calling on him.

'Had a message you were on your way to help sort this mess out and discover who killed Gordon Dugdale.'

'I hope I can anyway.'

Meade sat down and Cassidy poured out mugs of coffee for them both. 'Glad you're here as a matter of fact. I don't know who shot Gordy and with all else I've gotta do in town I ain't likely to find out either, yet Dugdale sends someone in nearly every day to ask how I'm getting on.' He shrugged. 'I guess I don't blame him. It was his son and heir who got murdered but badgering me won't help. He's also starting to make threats about punishing whoever did it and I doubt I could control him if he decided to carry 'em out. I hope you'll be able to stop him.'

Meade was aware of the young man looking at him somewhat doubtfully. He decided not to make any promises he might not be able to keep. He drank some of the coffee. It was hot and strong, the way he liked it.

'What can you tell me about what happened?'

'Gordy was shot on his way back to the ranch after a night spent in town, here in one of the cells actually, after he caused a ruckus in The Sycamore Stop. Gus Dugdale sent one of his hands in to fetch me and I went back out with him straight off, although it was getting too dark by the time I got there for me to do anything worthwhile till the following morning. Then I took a good look round but I couldn't find anything to show who'd done it.'

'Wasn't there anyone out at the ranch to help you read sign?'

'No, sir.'

'What about here in town?'

Cassidy shook his head. 'Not at the moment. There is a guy used to be an army scout who's still pretty good at following tracks and telling what they mean but he's gone with the sheriff looking for Apaches. You've heard about that I suppose? Iffen he'd been around I'd've used him for sure. He might well have found something I couldn't.'

Meade thought it was unfortunate such a chance had been lost. In his previous job as a marshal he had had some experience of following sign but there probably wouldn't be anything left after all this time. 'What else did you do?'

'I asked a few questions out at the ranch but no one had seen anyone acting suspiciously. Then I questioned one or two likely culprits here in town but naturally they all denied any wrongdoing. I ain't got any evidence against anybody. And I'm a town marshal not a detective. I've never had to deal with murder before.'

Nor had Meade.

'So, what was Gordon Dugdale like?' Meade finished his coffee and put the mug down on the desk.

Cassidy paused thoughtfully for a moment or two then said, 'Well, sir, he wasn't a bad lad, exactly, but he, like his pa, was inclined to strut around like he owned the town and believed that everyone in it should do what he wanted. He put people's backs up. Deliberately at times.

'He made enemies.'

Cassidy shrugged. 'Enough. He didn't care much about other people's opinions, especially if he took a dislike to someone.'

'And was there anyone in particular that he disliked?' Meade sat forward.

Cassidy didn't hesitate. 'Ralph Addington mainly. He's the one Gordy had a fight with in the saloon, iffen you can call it a fight. Ralph wasn't any match for him, which is why I had to put a stop to it with the butt of my gun.'

Meade hid a smile, thinking that Cassidy sounded as if he'd enjoyed using force on the young man.

'Ralph is a doctor and Gordy was always jealous of him, his schooling and his town manners. He took against Ralph as soon as he saw him. It was just one of those things I guess because

Ralph never boasted about his achievements or acted big. But it grated on Gordy that he had brains and that people respected him for that. None of the Dugdale family is high on book learning.'

'Is that what the fight was over?'

'No.' Cassidy got up to pour them both out more coffee. 'That was about Polly Murdock.' As he sat down again he leant forward with his arms on the desk and frowned. 'That was a real rotten business. Polly was the daughter of my deputy — '

'I thought you didn't have a deputy.'

'I don't. Not any more.'

Meade signalled for him to continue because whatever had happened to the deputy and his daughter was obviously an important part of the story.

'You see several years ago Murdock's wife died and he thought it would be best if little Polly went back East to live with his folks there. He hoped they could give her a better life and more opportunities. Anyway a few months ago Polly moved back out here to be with her pa, to see him again, for a while at least. She'd grown up, become a real pretty girl, and she quite turned Ralph's head. They started walking out with one another. Would've made a good match. So then Gordy suddenly ups and decides he loved Polly and wanted her for himself whereas I doubt that normally he would've taken any notice of her. She wasn't his type, being a nice girl and rather shy. Gordy preferred girls who knew what they were about. He just wanted to get one over on Ralph. He was good-looking and rich and could be polite and funny when it suited him and Polly was both a little naïve and ready to be swept off her feet by his promises and lies.'

'He seduced her?'

'That's right and of course the upshot was she found she was pregnant with his baby. Upon which he didn't want her any longer.'

Meade frowned. He didn't like hearing things like that.

Nor did Cassidy if the look on his face was anything to go by. 'The poor girl was devastated and so was her pa. Anyway Dugdale paid over a considerable amount of money to Murdock and they both left town in a hurry.'

'Will they come back?'

'I doubt it. Murdock was a proud man. And he loved his daughter and wouldn't want people laughing at or talking about her, which would be bound to happen despite the fact they felt sorry for her and mad at Gordy. You may be sure that Ralph, while a usually mild-mannered young man, was grievously unhappy about it all. I think he would've married Polly and given the baby his name but Polly was ashamed of treating him badly and being fooled by Gordy. She wanted to leave as much as her father.'

'Could Murdock have come back here to kill Gordon Dugdale for ruining his daughter?'

'I suppose so, yeah. But surely he would've done that at the time Gordy rejected Polly, not now, several months later.'

Meade frowned. 'The same could be said for Ralph Addington. Is he the one Dugdale suspects? The one he's making threats against?'

'Mostly, yeah.'

'Who else?'

'Well, there's Tony Vaughan who owns The Sycamore Stop. Gordy often got in a fight in the saloon and damage was done, although Dugdale always paid for any repairs. There's the fact too that whenever Gordy gambled there he cheated, which was bad for business.'

'And which would also give some of the other players a motive.'

Cassidy nodded. 'Even when stakes are low, feelings run high. Gordy also owed money all over.'

'That doesn't sound like much of a motive for murder.'

'I agree, especially as Dugdale eventually paid his son's debts. But you see, sir, here's the thing.' Cassidy leant back in his chair and stroked his chin.

'Apart from Ralph, it's highly unlikely that the murderer could have come from Sycamore Corner.'

'Why not?'

'The ranch is at least an hour's ride away and Gordy was killed near his home. That would mean the killer would have to be missing from town for several hours, especially if he rode out before Gordy so he could lie in wait for him. A shopkeeper couldn't've closed his place of business for an afternoon without it being remarked upon. And if Tony Vaughan hadn't been behind the bar he would've been missed too.'

'I see what you mean. Only Ralph Addington could ride out of town for that long with no one noticing because they would think he was somewhere tending to one of his patients.'

'Exactly.'

'Have you told Dugdale that?'

'Absolutely not. He's suspicious enough of Ralph as it is without me giving him more cause to act rashly.'

'But you think it more likely that the killer is employed out on the ranch? Or that maybe it's someone who works for a rival rancher?'

'That I do,' Cassidy said with a determined nod. 'I don't know much about either the cowboys at the Broken Spur or those who work on the other ranches round here except that they come into town to buy goods and equipment and often stay to drink and gamble. Sometimes they cause trouble, sometimes they don't. Gordy had his favourites who hung around with him until they annoyed him whereupon he ignored them. He could also be handy with his fists and I expect that if he played poker with any of 'em he cheated them too.'

'Cowboys can be a prickly lot.'

'I also know Dugdale fired anyone he thought wasn't pulling his weight so a dismissed cowboy could've killed the son to take revenge on the father.' He shrugged. 'And it's a fact Dugdale throws his weight around with the other ranchers as much as he does here in town.'

Meade gave a little sigh. He saw he was going to have his work cut out to find the killer.

'What are you going to do, Mr Meade?'

'First, I'd better go out to the Broken Spur and talk to Dugdale. Let him know I've arrived. Warn him not to do anything he might regret.'

'D'you want me to go with you?' Cassidy didn't sound too happy at the idea.

'No, I don't think so.' It was clear to Meade that Cassidy didn't much like the rancher and from what he could gather Dugdale didn't have much time for the town marshal. Best keep them apart if he could. 'I'll go first thing in the morning before it gets too hot. Can I hire a horse at the livery?'

'Yeah. And you'll need somewhere to stay in town. Your best bet is Mrs Darcy. She and her husband own the café across the way and they let out the couple of rooms above it. It's cheaper than the hotel and she provides decent food.'

'OK. I'll go across there now.' Meade stood up. 'I'll also need to speak to Addington. Perhaps you'd introduce me to him.'

'Be glad to. What about a drink in The Sycamore Stop this evening?'

'Good idea.'

'That way you can also talk to Tony Vaughan and his two girls before you see Dugdale. Find out what they thought of Gordy. And there was someone in the saloon gambling with him that you should know about. I'll let them tell you all about him because he was here and gone without me even seeing him.'

6

The Sycamore Stop was a fancy saloon with its name picked out in gold leaf on the two windows that fronted the sidewalk. Swing doors led into the large square room beyond, which had a wood floor and unpainted walls decorated here and there with paintings of cowboys and Indians. Lamps hung from the ceiling while tables and chairs dotted the centre of the room. Cassidy said Vaughan kept the place clean and served cold beer and decent whiskey, all of which meant the place was crowded in the evenings.

Tony Vaughan was a big man who now, in his late forties, was running to fat. He had brown hair with a bald spot in the middle and dark eyes behind spectacles he needed for shortsight.

As he poured out beers for the two men, he said, 'Gordy could be a pain in the ass at times. He always came in here when he was in town and he liked to play poker. He wasn't a good player and because he didn't like losing he cheated. He wasn't much good at cheating either and most everyone knew that's what he did.'

'I wonder that he found anyone to play with him,' Meade remarked. 'Or that he hadn't been called out for it.' In his experience most gamblers didn't like being cheated and were quick to pull a gun on those they suspected of the deed.

Vaughan paused in wiping a beer glass. 'Mostly you'd be right, Mr Meade, and very often he couldn't get anyone to join him in a game. But,' he shrugged, 'it wasn't usual for a lot of money to be involved. Gordy was so bad a player that despite him cheating there was always the chance of beating him. And I guess everyone knew that old man Dugdale would pay over the odds to anyone who complained they'd lost unfairly. Not that many dared do so,' he added.

'Dugdale seems to believe money solves everything.'

'That he does.'

'Was there anyone who took a particular dislike to Gordon's antics?'

'Not that I can think of,' Vaughan said with a glance at Cassidy, who shook his head in agreement. 'As I say, a number of men refused to play with him but I can't remember anyone, not even one of those who lost to him regularly, being angry enough they'd lay in ambush for him and shoot him dead.'

Cassidy added, 'They'd've challenged him here at the table.'

'True,' Vaughan agreed.

Meade finished his beer which was cold and refreshing and bought a fresh round for him and Cassidy.

'What about anyone else he angered? I understand from the marshal that he got drunk quite often and when that happened he lost his temper and liked to pick a fight with whoever was around at the time.'

'That's right,' Vaughan said. 'He caused a lot of damage to my place over the years but again Dugdale always paid up to have it put right, with usually quite a bit more to make up for the inconvenience. And I can't think of anyone he beat up bad enough he'd be killed for it. Can you, Sam?'

'No.'

'What about the girls who work here?'

'Angie and Christine.' Vaughan indicated the two prostitutes who were both talking to a group of townsmen. 'Angie is the elder of the two.'

She was a pretty young woman in her twenties with long black hair and black eyes. The other, Christine, seemed to giggle a lot and was much younger, only about seventeen, and quite plain with mousy brown hair pinned up in curls on top of her head.

'Angie is the one always went to bed with Gordy. He treated her OK but he could be a bit rough when the mood took him and for the moment I want to protect Christine who ain't been here long enough to know how to deal with any rough stuff. Angie could handle him and she never complained.'

'Would you have done anything if she had?'

'Yeah, Mr Meade, I would.' Vaughan's eyes glinted behind his spectacles.

'All right.'

Meade took him at his word, although he knew that saloon owners were often indifferent to what happened to the girls they employed. Anyway, it was highly unlikely that either of the prostitutes would have found the opportunity to ambush one of their customers, however violent he might have been and however much she might have wanted to do so. A prostitute's life wasn't her own.

'I think you've got something to tell me about a man in here who was playing cards with Gordon.'

'Winning too,' Vaughan said with a grin. 'Which didn't go down well. Especially as he was a Southerner.'

Cassidy leant against the bar and turning to Meade said, 'I dunno if you're aware of it or not but Gus Dugdale fought for the North in the Civil War. Was a general or some such. While he and his family moved out to Arizona soon after the fighting was over he's brought up his kids to dislike the South and everything about it and especially to dislike anyone he considers a traitorous Rebel.'

'Seems stupid to me after all this time.' Vaughan shrugged. 'Especially out here in Arizona which wasn't really affected by what went on in the East. You'd think he'd want to forget the fighting, wouldn't you?'

But Meade knew that for some, defeated or victorious, feelings still ran high.

'Tell me about this man. Do you know who he was?'

Vaughan shook his head. 'He was a stranger who just happened to be playing cards when Gordy came in. Unfortunately, there was just the one group playing that evening and so Gordy joined them which he probably wouldn't've done otherwise. I think he hated playing poker against a Southerner and only did so because he wanted to take the man down a peg or two and gloat over winning all his cash. It didn't work out like that because the Southerner proved to be a far better player and beat Gordy hollow.'

'He didn't like that,' Cassidy put in.

'No, he was in a real bad mood over it, especially as he lost quite a bit of money and he knew his pa would be none too pleased. Both about losing so much and over who he'd lost it to. He had one or two harsh things to say about the South even while the gambling was going on.'

'Enough to make the Southerner seek revenge?'

'Who knows?' Vaughan gave another shrug. 'Southerners can be quick to anger at times. Especially if their homeland is criticized or if they lost everything in the War. And he did look a proudful sort. It was a real stupid risk to take.'

'No one ever said Gordy had brains,' Cassidy mumbled.

'Where is this Southerner now?'

'He left town the next day,' Vaughan said. 'But after Gordy was hauled off to jail he took Christine upstairs and stayed the night. Hey, Chrissie.'

The girl looked up and when Vaughan beckoned to her she sashayed over to the men. She eyed Meade in a professional manner and seemed to like what she saw, smiling shyly at him.

'Chrissie, tell Mr Meade about the Southerner you took to bed the other night.'

'What would you like to know?' The girl placed a hand on Meade's arm.

'Did he tell you his name or anything about himself?'

'He said his name was Piers Laidlaw.' She wrinkled her brow in a frown. 'At least I think that's right cos it was a real strange name and he had a real strong accent. He was passing through the

West gambling an' such. He left me real early the next morning which was a pity.' Another shy smile. 'And he said he was heading out of town which was also a real pity. He was real nice. A gentleman.'

'Did he say where he was going next?'

'Umm, yeah, Leeville.'

'That's just on the far side of the hills,' Cassidy put in. 'Quiet place. No stagecoach goes there but it's right in the middle of some big ranches so it'd be a good place for a gambler to head.'

Christine went on, 'Mr Laidlaw said he'd been going on there anyhow but he had hoped to stay on in Sycamore Corner for a while first.'

'But he changed his mind?'

'Yes, Mr Meade, all because of that real awful Gordy Dugdale! And the real awful remarks Gordy made about him being from the South. When Mr Laidlaw won a third round of poker Gordy even threatened him. Said he'd ride back to the ranch and then fetch some men back here to string him up.'

'I doubt even Gordy would have gone that far,' Cassidy protested.

'Nor me,' Vaughan said.

Christine frowned. 'Well, Mr Laidlaw weren't to know that. It weren't that he was frightened of Gordy or his threats, just that he'd had enough of fighting in the War and now liked to live a real peaceful life and didn't want to get into any sort of trouble.'

In that case Meade thought it might have been better if he'd taken up some occupation other than gambling.

'There are a lot of people who feel the same way,' Vaughan put in. 'But Gordy and his pa wouldn't've understood that kinda attitude. Dugdales don't believe in turning the other cheek. Chrissie, can you tell Mr Meade anything else? Any more the man might've said?'

'No, Tony,' Christine said after a few moments thought. She put a hand on Meade's arm again. 'Can I do anything else for you?'

'Not just now,' Meade said with a smile.

With a little sigh of regret the girl wandered over to another man, who she obviously didn't consider anywhere near as handsome as the governor's man.

Vaughan wiped down the bar with a clean cloth and said, 'You know, Mr Meade, thinking about all this, it's possible that Gordy was still worked up enough to go after Laidlaw. I mean he seemed OK to me, had gotten over his bad temper an' all but who knows with someone like him. They could've had a fight and like he did in the gambling Gordy came off worst.'

'And the ranch is over in the direction of Leeville,' Cassidy added. 'Only problem is this Southerner left town a lot earlier than Gordy. But I guess they could've met up in the hills if Laidlaw had taken a stop to rest and Gordy came across him there and started up his remarks again. Like Tony says I wouldn't've put anything past that foolish young man.'

'Did you say anything about this Southerner to Dugdale?'

'God, no!' Cassidy said with a shiver of horror at the thought of what might have happened had he done so.

'Good. Let's keep it that way. Tony, another couple more beers then I'll head back for Mrs Darcy's.'

'On the house, gentlemen.'

As Cassidy left Meade at the café door, Meade said, 'I'll let you know how I get on at the ranch.'

'Good luck.'

Meade had the uncomfortable feeling he was going to need it.

7

Meade left Sycamore Corner the following morning after enjoying Mrs Darcy's breakfast, which was as good as her dinner had been the night before.

At the livery stable he hired a sturdy mare, who would, he was assured by the stable owner, complete the journey without any trouble. He also made sure he had a canteen filled with water.

The streets of the town were already busy as he rode away and he was aware of several people staring after him; obviously they knew from the town grapevine why he was here. Almost as soon as he left the place behind, certainly when he reached the far side of the sycamore grove that nearly encircled the town, he found himself on Dugdale land: the Broken Spur ranch.

Riding along he surveyed the landscape. Grass was sparse and there was little in the way of cattle. He decided that by this time of the year they would have been driven up into higher country. Neither did he see anyone, except once when he spotted a lone rider in the distance, who disappeared over the horizon even as he watched.

It was a lonely harsh land but near enough to water and the hills to make it good cattle country. Dugdale must have found it so anyway.

But because it was so open and empty then surely another horseman would be easy to spot. Meade thought that if someone from Sycamore Corner was Gordon Dugdale's killer then he must have ridden out here in advance of Gordon and lain in wait for him. Otherwise Gordon would have seen him or at least his dust. It might have meant a long, hot wait but the killer would know his quarry would leave town and come this way eventually. It also meant Cassidy was right when he said most townsmen would be missed if they were away from home or work for that long a time.

Except for Ralph Addington, the doctor, who worked just for himself, had no family, and could use the excuse that he was visiting patients to be away from his surgery. Even if his movements were checked up on, how accurately would ill people be able to remember what time they had been visited by the doctor or how long he had stayed? Or even what day it had been. Nevertheless, it was something he might have to ask Sam Cassidy to follow up if he hadn't done so already, which Meade didn't think he had. He had the idea that Cassidy wasn't taking the murder of Gordon Dugdale as seriously as he would have if Gus Dugdale had been more appreciative of him and his efforts, rather than behaving as if he believed the town marshal of little account.

Certainly, if Gordon had seen Ralph Addington he would have had no fear of him and not considered he posed a threat; until it was too late.

Meade was about halfway to the ranch when off to the right a vast range of hills came into view, rising from tree-covered foothills to slopes high enough to be considered mountains where little grew and whose jagged tops would be covered with snow in the winter. They were all part of Broken Spur land. Dugdale must have arrived before any other rancher and bought, stolen or somehow laid his hands on a prime position and prime land.

Cassidy said he should ride for the hills and the ranch headquarters were just on the other side. As he entered the trees they provided welcome shade from the beat of the sun and it became considerably cooler.

It was also around here that Gordon Dugdale had been killed. Probably somewhere close by, Meade thought, as he followed the trail around the bottom of a low, scrub-covered hill and a cluster of buildings appeared in the distance. He wondered why the killer had taken a risk in shooting Gordon down when he was almost home and he realized it was probably because here was about the only place along the whole trail where the killer could have lain in ambush without being seen by his victim.

He realized he'd been spotted.

Three riders were galloping in his direction. The men had their rifles out of their scabbards, held ready to use. Wisely, Meade pulled the mare to a halt and waited, hands well away from his own guns. The men stopped close to him and one of them, a hard-bitten man in his forties, came nearer.

'Who are you, mister? What d'you want here?'

'Jeremiah Meade from the office of the Governor of the Territory of Arizona. You should know about me. I'm here to see Mr Dugdale about the murder of his son, Gordon. I have a letter of introduction in my pocket.'

'Oh yeah,' the man said. 'We heard someone was on the way.' He put his rifle away indicating the other two should do the same and rode up to Meade, holding out his hand for Jeremiah to shake. 'Sorry about the guns. We're all a bit jittery just now.'

'That's understandable.'

'Dick Hoskins,' the man introduced himself. 'I'm the ranch foreman. Been with Mr Dugdale more or less ever since he came out here when I was just about as green as him. He's real shook up by this. So's the rest of the family. I surely do hope you can find the bastard who done it and quick.'

'I'll do my best.'

Hoskins looked as if that wasn't exactly the answer he expected but he said no more. He merely turned his horse and all four rode on together. Meade and Hoskins were a little ahead of the other two so Meade decided to take the opportunity to question the foreman.

'Could any of the hands at the ranch be responsible for Gordon's killing?'

Hoskins didn't answer for a moment and Meade wondered if he was angry at the suggestion. Then he said, 'It's quite possible. Gordy could be a silly sonofabitch at times. But offhand I can't think of anyone that he angered especially in the days up to the killing.'

'What about anyone who's been dismissed?'

'The last guy that happened to was three, four months ago now.'

'Or someone from the other ranches?'

'Could be.' Hoskins shrugged. 'Look, sir, I ain't being difficult on purpose. Christ, I've given all this a great deal of thought but I ain't been able to come up with the killer's identity much as I wish I could. Like Mr Dugdale, I think it's most likely someone from town. Gordy wasn't any too popular there. None of us is come to that. They consider us rabble-rousers, although they're eager to take our money.'

Which was a common complaint of cowboys.

As the buildings came closer Meade saw a couple of barns and a line of stables grouped around two large corrals, in which was some good horseflesh. There was a sturdy-looking bunkhouse and a separate hut for the foreman. Wood was stacked against the side of the barn. And some way off from the work area was the ranch house. It was two storeys high with a veranda all the way round, wide steps led up to the front door and the sash windows had glass in them. The house was shaded by sycamores and surrounded by colourful gardens.

The governor was right when he said Gus Dugdale had money. And lots of it.

But right now all the money in the world didn't amount to much, Meade thought, as they rode by a railed-off area. It contained a couple of graves, including a new, raw one topped with an elaborate tombstone, on which were inscribed the words, 'Gordon Charles Dugdale, 1856–1881, much loved son and brother, cut down in his prime'.

As the two cowboys peeled away from them, Hoskins said, 'I'll take you up to the house, sir. Mr Dugdale will be there. Since the shooting he ain't done much of anything except sit in his study. I'm worried 'bout him. I'm guessing he won't even start to get over this until the murderer is caught.'

Meade dismounted and followed the foreman up the steps and into the house. A corridor lined with paintings of Western landscapes led to a room that overlooked the ranch so Gus Dugdale could sit at his desk and watch the work that was going on.

Dugdale was in his early fifties. He had a head of thick, greying hair and blue-grey eyes. He was obviously a powerful man in word and deed, but as he stood up to shake Meade's hand it seemed to Jeremiah that he had recently shrunk, his clothes looking as if they no longer fitted him properly. Although still big and burly he was a pale imitation of the man he must have been a short while ago.

'Sit down.' Dugdale indicated the chair opposite him.

'May I offer you and your family my

condolences and those of the governor.'

'Thank you.' Dugdale poured out whiskey for them both, good whiskey in crystal glasses, and offered Meade a cigar, which he refused, lighting one up for himself. He swallowed the whiskey in one gulp and gave a slight shudder and quickly poured himself some more. 'I'm glad that at last the governor decided to send someone out here to help me find my boy's killer when the county sheriff obviously feels fighting Apaches miles away in Bisbee is more important. I was just about losing all patience with Cassidy, who does nothing but bleat on about how he can't do anything and doesn't know anything. Makes me wonder how the stupid bastard ever came to be elected marshal.'

Meade didn't think it was the right time or place to point out that Cassidy worked for the town, and seemed to be coping with that all right, and that he wasn't answerable to Dugdale. He felt sure Cassidy had said the same, many times before. The rancher wouldn't listen; he was the type of man who believed everyone should do their best for him right away when he wanted it done and put everything else second.

'Can you catch the goddamned murderer?' There was an anxious hope in the man's voice. 'Are you up to the job?'

'I'll certainly do all I can. Marshal Cassidy has given me the background to what took place.'

'Good. You know, Meade, my money's on that damned Ralph Addington.' Dugdale slammed his hand down on the table. 'He's a snob, always has been, and for some reason he's got it in for Gordy. Had I mean. Thinks he's better than me and mine. Jealous of us and our wealth too.'

'He's someone I intend to talk to. He's a possibility, especially as he was sweet on Polly Murdock and he was obviously upset over what happened to her.'

Dugdale had the grace to look uncomfortable at mention of the girl.

He even reddened. 'Listen, what my boy did to her wasn't right I'll grant you that but don't you go badmouthing him because of it. She should have known better than to give herself to him. My Celia never did me. It's not the man's fault when a girl can't take responsibility for herself. And if Ralph couldn't hold on to the girl he was meant to love then he's not much of a man and didn't deserve her.'

Meade bit down on an angry retort about Gordon only taking advantage of Polly to get at Ralph Addington. Dugdale wouldn't appreciate any outside criticism of his family, especially at the moment. He didn't want to antagonize the man unnecessarily.

'That aside, could the killer be someone from one of the other ranches around here? Or even one of your own men?' He asked the same questions he'd asked Hoskins.

Dugdale shook his head. 'No doubt some of the other ranchers are envious of the Broken Spur but I can't believe that any one of 'em would kill Gordy because I had more money and power than them. Why not kill me? And why do so now? This is settled land out here these days. As for the men I employ, no doubt Gordy treated one or two of 'em roughly but any who was dismissed because of something Gordy did or didn't do I made sure I paid off, and well, so they had no complaints.'

Practically everything in the man's life came down to money. It was his answer to all his problems and he would never understand that to other people money didn't necessarily make up for slights or wrongs.

'What about rustlers? Could one of them have come back to take revenge on you? Or perhaps it was a member of their family?'

'Maybe. I doubt it though. I admit that most of the rustlers we caught in the early days we strung up, but that was a long while ago now, and no one's been by looking for vengeance yet. And after Cassidy went back to town I had

Hoskins take some of the men and search the immediate area in case the bastard was hiding out watching the place. They didn't find a trace of anyone.'

Meade didn't point out that there was a lot of ground to cover out there and someone could have seen the searchers and slipped away without being seen himself. Dugdale would know that well enough.

'No, Meade, you look for the killer in that goddamned town. And you look good and hard at that goddamned doctor. It'll be him who's guilty. He wants stringing up and I've got the rope ready.'

Meade sat up straighter. He realized Dugdale was testing him and his resolve and he knew he had to take charge from the very start or the rancher would decide he could ride roughshod over him as easily as he thought he could the town marshal.

'I don't want you taking the law into your own hands, Mr Dugdale.'

'Going to stop me, are you? You're a

long way from Prescott.'

'I'll stop you if I have to. Whoever is guilty the law will punish them, not you. Understand?'

'OK, OK.' Dugdale held out his hands. 'You're right I suppose.' He sighed. 'Days when justice was swift and sure are long gone.' He sighed again obviously missing them.

Meade was satisfied. That was settled. He was the one in charge.

8

Dugdale stubbed out the remainder of his cigar. 'What do you intend to do first?'

'While I'm out here I'd like someone to show me the spot where your son was shot.'

'OK,' Dugdale agreed with a nod. 'Cassidy did take a look round but he didn't find anything.'

Meade couldn't decide whether the man was criticizing the marshal for his lack of success or him for wasting time doing something that had already been done. He took no notice. He would do this his way.

'Then I'll go back to town and question people there.'

'Let me know if you need any help.'

'I will.' But Meade doubted he would ask the rancher for help; that would probably be asking for trouble as well.

'I'll also want to question your men at some time.'

Again a nod of agreement, reluctant this time. Then Dugdale pulled a watch out of his vest pocket. 'It's just on time for our midday meal. Perhaps you'd like to join us and meet the rest of my family.'

'Yes, thank you.'

'Let me warn you, Meade, my wife is taking this real hard. The death, the murder of her first born . . . ' Dugdale was unable to go on, obviously as upset as his wife.

'Don't worry, sir, I'll be careful.'

At that moment there was an interruption with a knock on the door. It opened to reveal a woman in her thirties. Meade thought she was too young to be Celia Dugdale and as she said, 'Food's just about ready, sir,' her words quickly confirmed that she was obviously a servant. A servant! Dugdale sure had money.

'Thanks. We'll be right along. I trust there's enough for one more.'

'Of course, sir.'

Meade followed Dugdale out into the hall and along to a large, airy room at the side of the house. Even though it was hot outside it was pleasant in here, thanks to the floor-to-ceiling windows open on to the shade of the veranda. Scent from the flower garden outside drifted into the room on a slight breeze. Three people waited for them.

'Gus, there you are.' The woman came up to Dugdale and put an arm through his. She looked relieved to see him as if she didn't like letting him out of her sight and worried about him all the time he was gone from her side.

'Mr Meade, this is my wife, Celia.'

She was a year or so younger than her husband and would have been good-looking were it not for her red-rimmed eyes and puffy cheeks. A glint of fear lingered on her face. She was dressed from head to toe in black, a colour that didn't suit her, making her look too pale and thin. It was clear she was holding herself together with some difficulty and when Meade shook her hand he felt her trembling.

'We're so thankful you're here, Mr Meade. Now whoever killed my darling boy will be brought to justice.' She wiped her eyes on a lace-edged handkerchief.

'Don't cry, dear.' Dugdale patted her hand, grimacing as though he wished he could find some way to comfort her but didn't quite know how. 'And this is my son, Louis, and my daughter, Ella.'

Louis stood over by one of the windows, seeming to melt into the background, rather than involving himself in what was going on. He was of middle height and like his mother had fair hair, blue eyes and a light complexion that obviously burnt in the sun. There was a discontented air about him and Meade couldn't decide if he was shy, bored or simply uninterested. Or something else entirely.

Ella was about nineteen and quite beautiful. Her brown hair hung in waves halfway down her back and she had grey eyes and rosy cheeks and a voluptuous figure enhanced by the tight-fitting dress she wore. She was very aware of the impression she made as she held out her hand for Meade to shake. Doubtless she thought it was her right that every man she met worshipped at her pretty feet. Meade might easily have done so when he was younger but now he was much too old for her and had anyway seen any number of beautiful women.

'We miss Gordy so much,' she said going to stand on her mother's other side. 'None of us can think of any reason for anyone to kill him. It's all made so much worse by not knowing who did it or why.'

'I did wonder if it was some kind of madman or maybe even Indians. There hasn't been any Apache trouble out here for a while but there are always renegades . . . ' Celia's voice trailed away.

'Now, dear, we've been through all this before and you know either possibility is most unlikely. Don't you agree, Meade?'

'I doubt it was anyone like that. But I'll keep an open mind until I find out more.'

'Louis.' Dugdale called to his son who was half-turned to look out of the window. There was a slight irritation in his voice. 'Louis, Mr Meade wants to visit the canyon where your brother was shot. Will you take him there?'

Louis spoke for the first time. 'After we've eaten, sir?'

'Yes, that's fine. Afterwards I can continue on back to town.' Meade hoped Dugdale wouldn't object to that for he had no real wish to remain at the ranch intruding on these people and their grief, or giving them what could well turn out to be false promises about his ability to catch the killer.

The family employed at least one other servant, a young girl of about sixteen who fetched in the food and stayed to serve it. 'Is everything satisfactory, sir?' she asked before

Dugdale dismissed her with a wave of his hand. No one else had taken any notice of her except for Louis who gave her a slight smile of thanks as she put his plate on the table before him.

The food was hot and plentiful but rather too fancy for Meade's taste. He preferred his steak well done and not covered with sauces. But at least he ate his meal which was more than could be said for the others, except Louis he noted. Dugdale ate the meat and potatoes but little else and both Celia and Ella pushed the food around their plates, hardly eating any of it.

Conversation was desultory as well. Louis and Celia said nothing and after Ella had asked Meade what he thought of Sycamore Corner and the ranch she lapsed into silence. Dugdale quizzed him on the local political situation in Prescott and Arizona politics generally but it was obvious he didn't much care about any of it, which was quite understandable in the circumstances. It was a relief when the maid came in to clear the table and Meade could be on his way.

As Louis got to his feet Celia reached a hand out towards him, 'Be careful out there, please.'

'Isn't he always?' Ella said making Louis redden. 'I'm sure he'll come to no harm in Mr Meade's company.'

'The rest of us aren't in any danger are we, Mr Meade?' Celia asked.

'Oh, Mama, I didn't mean that.' Ella was conscience-stricken at having frightened her mother.

'No, I doubt it,' Meade tried to reassure the woman.

Dugdale accompanied Meade and Louis outside. 'Forgive my wife. She never used to be so nervous, not even when we first came out here and had trouble with Apaches, but now she's just so upset over Gordy and scared for the rest of us.'

'I understand. I'm sure she has nothing to worry about but it wouldn't do any harm to take precautions.'

'I am doing so. Good luck, Mr

Meade. Maybe I'll send someone in to town tomorrow to find out how you're getting on.'

'Give him a chance, Pa,' Louis spoke in an exasperated tone.

Dugdale ignored him. And as Meade followed Louis down the steps he had the feeling that the young man was used to being ignored.

Meade's horse had been well looked after. Hoskins ran the ranch efficiently and well. Meade waited while Louis saddled a brown gelding. Then watched by a couple of cowhands they rode out on to the trail. It was very hot, the sun glaring down out of a metallic blue sky, in which there wasn't a single cloud, making the air breathless.

As Louis didn't seem inclined to say anything, after a while Meade broke the silence. 'This good cattle country?'

'Guess so. Pa does all right anyway.'

'Now Gordon is dead I suppose you'll inherit it all.'

Louis flashed Meade a scornful look, in which there was underlying anger and bitterness as well. 'There were occasions when I didn't have much time for my brother, I admit that, but he was my brother. If you think I'd kill him for the Broken Spur ranch you're very much mistaken. I didn't shoot Gordy, I had no reason to.'

'You don't want to inherit the ranch?'

'I never said that, Mr Meade, not exactly. I grew up always expecting that Pa would ensure I'd have some say in its running.'

How much would obviously have depended on Gordon.

'Now he expects that I'll take it all on when the time comes for him to retire.' Louis shrugged. 'That's OK, I guess. Nowadays it doesn't really take all that much running anyway, especially with Hoskins in charge.'

'But you'd rather be doing something else?'

'I never said that either,' Louis said angrily. 'Don't put words in my mouth.'

But looking at him Meade decided that however much he might protest

Louis was unhappy with his lot in life, especially now when he was suddenly heir to a ranch and a way of life he seemed not to want. Did his father notice, or care? Or had Louis, the middle child, always been the odd one out? For it was obvious that Dugdale had loved his eldest boy and worshipped his daughter whereas it hadn't been easy to tell what he thought of his remaining son; or what Louis thought of him.

Perhaps the young man had become so fed up with the situation that he'd shot his brother in a fit of temper but Meade thought that unlikely, especially as Louis must have known his brother's death would resolve nothing but just make things more difficult for him.

'Here we are.' Louis pulled his horse to a stop at the bottom of a hill covered with rocks and scrub. He dismounted and Meade followed suit. 'Gordy's body was found roundabout here.' He indicated a dusty patch of ground. 'He was almost home.'

It was a good spot for an ambush with plenty of cover for someone to hide. Even now in the bright light of afternoon with the sun almost overhead there were still patches of shade where the hill met the canyon floor. Later on the shade would be edging into blackness. An ambusher lying in wait even quite close by wouldn't be seen, especially by a rider not expecting anyone to be there. And Gordon had been taken so completely by surprise he hadn't even had time to draw his gun, which Cassidy said was still in his holster.

'Marshal Cassidy came out here and searched the whole canyon. Whatever Pa might think or say about him he was real thorough. He's a good lawman. But he found no sign of whoever did it.'

Meade walked up and down the trail knowing he wouldn't find anything either. The ground was baked dry and was too hard for any prints to show up. The killer had left nothing behind him. He returned to where Louis waited with the two horses.

'How did you know something was wrong?'

'Gordy's horse came home without him. Hoskins raised the alarm. A few of us rode out to look for him.' Louis's eyes took on a faraway look. 'When we got here the shadows had stretched almost the whole way across the canyon. It was quite dark. We didn't see Gordy at first. Then Pa spotted him.' Remembering, he shivered. 'It was clear he was dead and nothing could be done for him. We took him home and Hoskins rode into town to alert the marshal.'

'Do you know what puzzles me?'

'No, what?'

'If the killer ambushed your brother rather than followed him from Sycamore Corner he would have had to lie in wait for him here.'

Louis looked puzzled wondering what Meade was getting at.

'Well, how did the killer know Gordon was on his way back from town and would reach here when he did?'

Louis gave a short, unamused laugh. 'Mr Meade, Gordy was a creature of habit. He always went into Sycamore Corner a couple of times a month, always on a Thursday, and he always stayed the night, coming back later the next day, getting home sometime during the afternoon. The killer might have had a long wait but he'd have known it wouldn't be in vain. But Pa is of the opinion that the killer followed him out from town.'

'Is that what you think?'

Louis shrugged. 'I don't know.'

'No, nor do I.'

'I hope you find whoever was responsible, for Ma's sake especially.'

'Same here.'

'Is that all, sir?'

There seemed little point in asking Louis anything more. So Meade nodded. 'For now. I'll be in touch.'

9

Was Mr Jeremiah Meade from the governor's office going to pose a problem? Maybe. But it didn't really matter. There was more than one way to deal with him.

* * *

Ralph Addington lived on the edge of Sycamore Corner in a house surrounded by a white picket fence. The place was big enough that rooms at one side served as a doctor's surgery and bedrooms where, if necessary, poorly patients could stay while they recovered from whatever ailed them.

'I could never understand why Polly chose Gordy over Ralph,' Cassidy said as he pushed open the gate and led the way up the path. 'Except I suppose Gordy was more exciting. More dangerous.'

Meade had long given up trying to fathom out why people behaved as they did. Ralph had loved Polly, and she him, until Gordon Dugdale came on the scene and enticed her away. Yet surely Ralph could offer her almost as much as the rancher's son in the way of comfort and position. Cassidy was probably right and Ralph had seemed staid and settled beside the more flamboyant Gordon. Her choice certainly hadn't done her any good.

'Ralph must be in; that's his buggy.' Cassidy indicated the vehicle standing in the dusty lane next to the house.

Ralph proved to be about twenty-nine, of medium height and quite stocky. His hair was light brown and his eyes brown.

Even though the Dugdales probably had more money than he did — small-town doctors hardly earned a fortune — and certainly, despite the respect doctors earned, the ranchers had more power in the community, Meade thought he could see why Gordon might be jealous of Ralph. For the young man had an intelligent face, was dressed in good quality store-bought clothes and carried himself well. He had an air of competence about him, which came from a good education and a good job, and his home was pleasant and well furnished.

He didn't look particularly pleased to see the two men and invited them into the parlour with some reluctance.

'I've been over this more than once with Marshal Cassidy,' he said, impatience in his voice. 'I was home for most of the morning recovering from the beating Gordon Dugdale gave me. A beating Cassidy didn't think bad enough to charge Gordon over. He believed a night in the cells was enough.'

'It was, especially as I had it on good authority that you started the fight.'

'Started it! Yes, with provocation!'

Meade interrupted. 'Did you see anyone in the morning who could confirm you were here?'

'No. I pinned a notice to the door saying I was cancelling my morning surgery. I didn't feel up to it nor did I think it would look good advising other people on their aches and pains when I was full of them myself.'

'Did you stay indoors all day?'

Ralph sighed. 'By the afternoon I'd recovered enough that I took the buggy out to Basset's farm to see Mrs Basset who is expecting another baby and hasn't been very well.'

'Do you know what time you got there and when you left?'

'I wasn't exactly looking at my watch every second of the day but it was well past noon when I left here, the farm is about thirty minutes drive away and I stayed for — oh, I don't know — an hour I suppose.'

'Can Mrs Basset confirm that?'

'If you ask her, yes, I'm sure she can.'

'Perhaps you'd ride out there and do just that,' Meade said to Cassidy, who nodded. Meade was aware that Ralph didn't look unsettled by what he suggested. Did that mean he was telling the truth or that he was a good actor, or maybe that he had been out to tend to Mrs Basset but stayed only a short while, leaving her in time to get to the canyon to kill Gordon, and that he hoped she wouldn't realize or remember how little time he had actually spent with her?

'Look, Mr Meade, I admit I had good reason to dislike Gordon Dugdale.' Ralph spread his hands. 'He's always disliked me too and we mostly kept out of one another's way but sometimes it was inevitable that we'd meet. Sycamore Corner is only a small place. And after the way he treated Polly you could say I hated him. You've heard about Polly I suppose?'

Meade nodded.

'But I didn't ambush him. If I'd wanted to shoot him I would have done it long since and I would have called him out here in town and faced him down like a man. I'm not a coward. But I didn't do that either because I'm a doctor, trained to save life not to take it. And shooting Gordon wouldn't have helped Polly in her predicament or brought her back here to me.'

'Would you have her back?'

'Yes.'

'Do you ever hear from her?'

'No.' Ralph shook his head. A look of deep unhappiness crossed his face. 'I wish I did. I never blamed her.'

Meade thought that was easy to say but he also thought that Ralph meant it. 'But you did blame Gordon?'

'Of course I did. Who else? He seduced Polly deliberately not because he loved her but to get back at me. Believe me there were times I wanted to shoot the bastard. But I didn't. Go speak to Mrs Basset please, you'll find I'm telling the truth.'

'Why did you come out West to practice as a doctor? You'd have made a lot more money if you'd remained in the East.'

Ralph smiled. 'Why does anyone come out West? For the thrill of it, the weather, freedom from society's rules?' He shrugged. 'Who knows? I like it here and I've never regretted my decision.'

Meade hoped he wouldn't have cause to regret it now, which he might do if Dugdale refused to believe him innocent of his son's killing.

'Now is that all? I'm quite busy you know.' Ralph stood up.

Meade stood up as well. He didn't see any way to get Ralph Addington to change his story and besides he was inclined to believe him.

'I really can't see Ralph as a dry-gulcher,' Cassidy said when he and Meade had returned to his office. 'And he's right. He would've had plenty of chances before now to challenge Gordy.' He sat down. 'So would anyone else Gordy annoyed.'

'Then something must have happened that made it necessary for the killing to take place when it did.'

Cassidy shrugged. 'I ain't aware of anything special, not here in town anyway.'

'And Dugdale didn't mention anything happening out on the ranch.'

'Mebbe something took place there that Dugdale don't even know about.'

'But it must be something important enough to kill over. And Dugdale seems the sort to keep his eye on everything to do with the ranch. Or at least depend on his foreman to tell him.'

'Yeah, you're right. Hoskins keeps Dugdale informed of all that's going on. Those two go way back and are more like friends than employer and employee.' Cassidy shrugged again. 'You can see why I never got anywhere with solving the murder, can't you?'

'That I can.' Meade's eyes narrowed. 'The only thing different I can come up with is that Southerner in the saloon, Piers Laidlaw.'

'I did wonder about riding over to Leeville to question him but it meant taking more time away than I could afford.'

Meade sighed. 'I'd better do that.

The first thing is to find out if he's still there.'

'Unfortunately, there ain't no telegraph line that goes there.'

That meant another long ride!

Cassidy grinned in sympathy then said, 'It ain't too bad a journey. It's mostly through the hills so it won't be too hot.'

'Good. I'll go later on this afternoon. It depends on what I find there on what time I get back.'

Cassidy got up to pour them out coffee and when he sat down again he said, 'Of course, it could be someone out at the Broken Spur with a secret reason of his own for killing Gordy that neither Dugdale or Hoskins has cause to suspect.'

'I know,' Meade said, thinking about Louis Dugdale.

'How did you get on out there?'

'I didn't discover anything of any real use,' Meade admitted. 'Probably no more than you know already.' He paused. 'Sam, what do you make of

Louis Dugdale?'

Cassidy leant back in his chair to ponder for a moment or two.

'For a start he's completely different from Gordy. Completely different from the others in the family come to that, except for his mother. Not that I know much about Mrs Dugdale because she rarely comes to town but when she does she's always polite and quiet, rather shy in fact, and Louis certainly takes after her in looks whereas Gordy and Ella favour the father.'

'I noticed that.'

'Louis doesn't play around with the ladies nor does he gamble.' Cassidy held out his hands. 'Not that he's a saint who never does wrong. I mean he goes into the saloon for a drink or two, he might even sleep with a prostitute now and then, but he doesn't play anyone false.'

'What about friends?'

Cassidy paused to think again. 'He doesn't seem to have any, not here in town anyway, and I can't see that he would make friends among his father's cowhands. Not that he's a snob but more so because rumour has it that he's not real happy out on the ranch and would like to do something else with his life.'

'That was my impression too, although he denied it. Have you any idea what he'd like to do instead?'

Cassidy shook his head. 'I doubt he knows himself because I imagine Dugdale expected both of his sons would follow him into the cattle business and probably wouldn't have countenanced either one doing anything different.'

'Louis said as much to me and admitted that now of course he'll certainly be expected to take over the running of the ranch.'

'Yeah, not something to look forward to if it's not what he wants.'

'How did he and Gordon get on? Do you know?'

'OK, I guess, although they rarely came to town together or spent much time doing the same things. But as far as I'm aware there were no out and out disagreements between 'em nor animosity either.' Cassidy frowned. 'Ella certainly preferred Gordy to Louis and made little secret of that fact and so did Dugdale. Gordy was a man's man and just like his father, Louis isn't. Even so they were a family and as such seemed to rub along together OK.'

'So Louis wouldn't have any reason to kill his brother?'

'Hell, no!' Cassidy looked quite shocked. 'I can't see Louis doing something like that. His own brother! No.' He shook his head again. 'Jeremiah, unless he's good at pretence I would say he's a gentle soul who always seems the odd one out in that family. I can't remember ever hearing that he's drawn a gun on anyone or even been much of a scrapper.' He grimaced. 'I suppose it might just be possible that he would shoot his brother in the heat of an angry moment but I'm sure there's no way he'd've planned it and carried it out in the cold-blooded way it was done.'

'You're probably right,' Meade agreed. 'Trouble is that goes for almost anyone doesn't it?'

10

Feeling better now that someone with more authority than a town marshal was investigating his son's murder, Dugdale decided it was time to get back to work. He'd neglected the paperwork necessary to run a large ranch and he hoped that by working he might find a way to control his grief and anger. And, by God, if he was going to do some work around the place so was Louis, who had spent the last few days in more of a mope than usual. There were times he wondered what on earth was wrong with the boy and what he was going to do with him. He'd never had problems with Gordon, who, whatever else might be said about him, could never be accused of not pulling his weight.

So just as the family was finishing breakfast, Dugdale put down his knife and fork and fixed Louis with a steely glance. Daring him to disagree, he said, 'Perhaps you'd best stir yourself and do something around the ranch today. Sort it out with Hoskins.'

'Are you sure that's a good idea?' Celia said anxiously.

'It's not good to be idle for too long and we must set an example to the hands.'

Knowing that her husband, especially when he frowned like that, was unlikely to change his mind she turned to Louis, holding out a hand towards him. 'Be careful, dearest.'

'I will, Ma, don't worry.'

'I'm sure Louis is in no danger,' Ella said, smiling sweetly at her brother. 'Unlike poor Gordy, Louis never misbehaves or gets into trouble, do you?'

'I try my best not to.'

Louis was aware she was not trying to support him but was actually trying to make trouble for him with their father, by making him out to be a mother's boy. He was determined not to be rattled by her and instead make allowances because he knew that Gordon had always been her favourite brother, the one she copied, the one she had always run after and wanted to be like. They had been alike in looks, temperament and personality. He, Louis, came a very poor second where she was concerned.

All the same he was angry with his sister. Her pointless fault-finding with him was upsetting their mother and he wanted to tell Ella she should think first of her and second of herself. He didn't bother, aware that it would cause more of a row because Ella wouldn't listen to him any more than Gordon had ever done.

Before his father could be goaded into losing his temper, he said, 'Sure, Pa, I'll go and talk to Hoskins.'

He sighed. It was unlikely the foreman would have anything he really wanted him to do. The cowhands could handle any work better than Louis. But for Dugdale's sake the man would find something.

Before Ella could say any more he stood up and left the room, getting his hat and his gun, and walked down to the corrals. He found Hoskins in the barn, supervising its cleaning out, a job he got the men to do regularly, however much they hated it.

Hoskins thought for a moment or two then said, 'Yeah, there is a job needs doing. Ride out into the hills and make sure everything's OK in the valley where we drove the cattle. You know where that is, don't you, even though you didn't come with us?'

Louis nodded, ignoring Hoskins' barb. Maybe his mother would be unhappy if she knew he was leaving the confines of the ranch but he felt hemmed in here, hardly able to breathe, and the job would keep him away from the ranch for much of the rest of the day which suited him fine.

'Young Tommy Walker is there keeping an eye on things. You can talk to him about whether there's enough grass and how long it'll last before we need move 'em again. Find out if he thinks anything else needs doing and also how he's coping out there on his own. Tell him I'll get one of the others to take his place within a day or two.'

Tommy had only been working for the ranch since the start of the summer and was just eighteen. Even so he was experienced enough to be put in charge of the cattle because Louis knew Hoskins would never have entrusted him with the task if he hadn't believed him up to it.

Hoskins relented a little in his hard attitude. 'You want anyone to go with you? In the circumstances.'

'No.' Louis could just imagine what his father and Ella would have to say about him wanting a nursemaid; he'd never live it down. Anyway, he was looking forward to being on his own when he would have a chance to be quiet and think and maybe rest awhile and look at the scenery. They were also things his father and Ella would never understand, although he felt his mother would, that she often did the same.

'Watch yourself.' Hoskins added his warning to Celia's.

It was another hot day but when Louis rode up into the foothills the going became easier. Some shade from the pines and cottonwood trees, even a little breeze, made it cooler. The trail led ever upwards through trees and round outcrops of rock, skirting thick undergrowth. Birds sang in the branches, a lizard dozed in the sun on top of a boulder.

Despite all its discomforts Louis liked Arizona, seeing it not with his father's eyes merely as cattle country, but beautiful in its colours and contrasts: the hot dusty desert, which bloomed with flowers in the spring rain, the high mountains where snow stayed on the peaks all year round. The strange vegetation and sometimes stranger animals. He felt he could live here quite happily were it not for having to work on the ranch.

But today he was too preoccupied to

enjoy the sights and sounds.

He had the uncomfortable feeling that Jeremiah Meade suspected him of killing Gordon, which was ridiculous, because it was also extremely ridiculous to imagine that he wanted the Broken Spur for himself. Of course his father had always taken it for granted that once he died and the ranch passed to Gordy, Louis would stay to help his brother. But Louis had always known that when that happened Gordy would have little time or use for him and wouldn't do anything to prevent him leaving.

Gordy was a prideful sort of man who had always felt he could run the Broken Spur better than his father. Unfortunately, he also made enemies because he had only ever thought of himself and what he wanted. But Gordy was his brother, they'd had good times together especially when they were younger, and Louis wished he wasn't dead. And wished too that whoever had killed him would soon be caught. It was destroying the family not knowing the who or why. It was especially hard on his mother. He wanted to do more to comfort her but at the moment no one could reach her and Louis was afraid she might never recover from her loss.

She had always made the best of her life out here. Tried not to show how scared she was at times with the harsh nature of both the land and those who peopled it. Pretended not to know the ruthless way Dugdale acted to protect what he had grabbed for himself. But it had all taken its toll on her and if Dugdale had been a different kind of man, more considerate of others' feelings, he would have noticed it too.

But now his father was also suffering with the loss of his elder son and while Louis didn't often feel sorry for him he did so now.

He just hoped Mr Meade was clever enough to figure out who the guilty party was and strong enough to stop Dugdale from taking the law into his own hands. Otherwise there would be more trouble ahead than any of them wanted or could handle.

And now Gordy was dead, where did that leave Louis? How could he let his father down? Yet how could he face staying here doing something he didn't want to? When all he longed for was to escape. The other problem was he didn't know what he really wanted to do with his life or where he wanted to go. Unlike Ralph Addington he didn't have much in the way of schooling beyond what was necessary for running a ranch.

He was halfway to the valley when he heard a sound. A rustling in the undergrowth, which made him think of an animal — perhaps a coyote, maybe even a cougar attracted by the nearby cattle. It was quickly followed by another noise.

And that was man-made.

Hell! What was it?

It came again. An ululating yell. Shivers ran up and down Louis's spine and his horse skittered backwards in alarm. It was probably that which saved his life. For at that very second shots came from close by — one, two, three. And all three bullets hit him. In the arm, the shoulder and high up in the chest.

In disbelieving shock Louis cried out and fell off his horse. Everything went black, the very air seeming to whirl around him. As he landed on the ground a tremendous pain hit him and he groaned.

But somehow he wasn't dead!

Not yet.

He glanced towards the trees and bushes from where the shots had come and saw movement there. He would be dead soon if he didn't do something, because he had no doubt that this was the same ambusher who had shot his brother and who wouldn't hesitate to finish him off from close range as he had Gordy.

Not sure whether he felt the pain or fear the most, but every instinct telling him he had to ignore both and get away, Louis rolled into the undergrowth on his side of the trail. Gritting his teeth against the scream at the throbbing that threatened to engulf him, somehow he crept forward on his stomach. Behind him he could hear the killer coming after him. He wouldn't get away, he couldn't . . .

Suddenly there directly in front of him, close to the edge of the path, was the slope of the hill. It wasn't very steep but he could do nothing to stop himself from tumbling over it and then rolling down it, jolts of pain searing through him, until he managed to grab at the roots of a bush and drag himself to a halt, crying out as agony jarred his whole body and sweat almost blinded him. He crawled under the bush and lay still, breathing hard, fighting desperately against swooning.

Was he well hidden? Surely the killer would see the blood, see where he'd tumbled down the hillside. None of it mattered because he couldn't move any further. He just had to crouch there, afraid and trembling, out of sight for the moment, and hope for the best. Hope that the killer wouldn't come after him but would believe that Louis, shot so many times, had to be dead.

* * *

The killer stopped at the top of the slope, looking down, holding the rifle ready. Louis should be dead and lying right there on the trail. Three times the killer had fired and three times the bullets struck the young man's body. Yet somehow he had crawled away from the path and from the looks of things fallen down the slope.

The killer wondered whether to go down there after him, finish him off. But time was passing by and more time would be wasted in searching for someone who was probably dead already, or would soon be.

And Louis was out here in the hills, all alone, and no one at the ranch would miss him for quite a while. He

114

would certainly be dead by the time he was found. And it would worry that bastard, Dugdale, all the more if his son was reported as missing and couldn't be found. Good!

That decided, the killer strode quickly away, shaking with excited laughter.

★ ★ ★

With a little moan Louis let out the breath he'd been holding. He'd been too scared and hurt to raise his head to try to see whoever had ambushed him, not wanting to make any movement that might give his position away. Now that it seemed the imminent danger was over, he was aware of the pain taking over every inch of his body, so bad he didn't know which part of him hurt the most.

He rested his head on the ground, hardly able to believe he was still alive. So now what should he do?

And with that thought Louis sank into unconsciousness.

11

After leaving Cassidy to get on with some marshal's business, Meade decided to walk down to the livery stable and hire a horse. He would need one for a couple of days at least and he hoped the mare would still be available. Then he'd have something to eat at the café before setting out for Leeville. He hoped that Piers Laidlaw would prove to be guilty but somehow he doubted it. It was too convenient and he was sure the answer lay closer to home.

He had the uncomfortable feeling that he was going to fail in finding Gordon Dugdale's killer, which wouldn't please him, Dugdale or the governor. Meade didn't like to fail but there didn't seem to be anything much to go on or to find out. Plenty of people had reason to shoot Gordon but few had the opportunity.

A buckboard stood outside the dry

goods store, a woman who looked vaguely familiar standing by the horses' heads. As he got closer Meade recognized her as the cook out at the Broken Spur. Just then the door to the shop opened and a girl struggled out carrying several heavy-looking parcels.

As she went to step from sidewalk to road she tripped and with a little cry fell over. She dropped her packages and landed on the ground in the middle of them, in a jumble of arms and legs.

'Katie!' The older woman gave a shout of alarm and started round the side of the buckboard.

Meade was there before her. He bent down, helping the girl, Katie, to sit up. 'Are you all right?'

'Yeah, I think so,' she said. 'I'm not sure what happened.' She tried to get up and with a grimace cried out, 'Ow! My ankle!' She sank back down on the ground, holding her foot.

'Are you badly hurt?' the woman asked, anxiety in her voice. 'Do you need Doc Addington?'

'It's my ankle, Ma.'

'Let me look.' The woman crouched down by her daughter and ran a hand over the girl's foot. 'I don't think it's broken. You've probably sprained or twisted it. You'll be OK in a minute or two.'

'Sit still for a while,' Meade added.

Katie seemed suddenly to become aware that several people had stopped to gawp. She put her head in her hands. 'Oh Lord, I feel such a fool. Why did I have to trip? I don't know how I did.'

'You were carrying too much, that's why,' her mother said. 'I said I'd come in and help you. You should have taken more notice of me.'

'I'm sorry,' Katie said tearfully. 'Now look at everything.' She indicated the parcels lying on the ground. 'At least nothing's breakable.'

'Don't worry,' Meade said. 'Rest there. I'll pick all these things up for you.' He began to gather together the packages and place them in the back of the buckboard. There were quite a lot of them. In between doing so he shooed away the bystanders and before long, realizing there was going to be no more excitement, they all drifted away.

'Thank you,' the woman said, as Meade put down the last of the parcels and made sure they were all secure. 'Oh! You're Mr Meade aren't you? You were at the Broken Spur yesterday.'

'That's right.'

'You're going to find whoever killed poor young Mr Gordon.'

Meade thought he was going to try.

'I'm Maybelle Bowen by the way and this is my daughter, Katie.'

Both women were of medium height with slender figures, brown hair and brown eyes. But whereas Katie was a pretty girl, her mother's face was creased with worry lines and she had an unhappy look lurking in the back of her eyes.

'I'm the cook out at the ranch,' Maybelle went on. 'While Katie helps me in the kitchen and serves at the table.'

'Pleased to meet you.'

'Thank you for your help, Mr Meade.' Maybelle turned to Katie. 'How are you now, honey?'

'All right, Ma.'

'Here, let me help you.' Meade put an arm around the girl's waist and helped her stand up.

She winced as she put her foot on the ground but then after a moment or two managed to put her weight on it. 'It feels OK.'

Maybelle eyed her daughter anxiously. 'Still we'd better not start back for the ranch just yet. It's such a long way. Why don't we go and have something to eat first? Afterwards you should be ready for the drive.'

Meade immediately decided to put off hiring a horse until later on and instead ask the two women a few questions about the ranch.

He said, 'I was going to the café myself. Why don't I treat you to dinner?'

'Oh no, you don't have to do that,' Maybelle protested.

'My pleasure.' And it would be as well, to have two good-looking ladies sitting at his table.

'Then thank you.'

With Meade supporting Katie, who limped a little, the three of them went back down the road to Mrs Darcy's café. Although there were already a number of customers inside enjoying a meal, they found a table by the window so they could look out on the street. They all ordered beef stew and apple pie.

As they waited for the food, Meade said, 'How long have you worked at the Broken Spur?'

'Not long,' Maybelle said, with a little frown. 'About four months now.'

'Nearer to six, Ma.'

'Why goodness me, yes, Katie, you're right. My, how time does fly!'

'Where are you from?' Meade was finding it difficult to place their accent.

'Denver. At least that's where Katie was born. I'm from a small town near Chicago originally. I came out West with my husband soon after we were married. When my husband died four years ago I decided we should return East to my family. I thought it would be best for Katie. And I was lonely too and wanted to be near my folks. But we didn't like it, did we, honey?'

The girl shook her head. 'It was so crowded. So many people and buildings and vehicles. Ma's family was nice enough but they all had families of their own and couldn't really look after us.'

'Once Katie was fifteen and old enough to leave school we headed West again in the hope we could find some work together out here. We weren't really sure where we were going to end up . . . '

'California sounded nice,' Katie said a little wistfully.

Maybelle smiled at her. 'While we were in Tucson we heard from someone who knew the Dugdales that Mr Dugdale needed a cook and a maid to help his wife. I've always liked cooking and I'm pretty good at it too and we decided to apply in the hope that we'd suit the family. So far we seem to do so and it suits us too, although it is a bit lonely out there being so far from town.' Maybelle spooned up some of the gravy on her plate. 'Umm, this is pretty good stew.'

Katie said, 'It's a real pretty place and everyone is so friendly.'

Meade had gained the impression that the family weren't all that friendly with any of their employees, except for maybe the foreman, but he let that pass. Perhaps Katie meant the cowhands were friendly because they must be counting their blessings at having two pretty girls out at the ranch and to count them even more because one was an employee like them and not another daughter of the ranch owner. It would be possible to flirt with Katie whereas it wouldn't be with Ella. And for one or two of the older men, such as Dick Hoskins, Maybelle Bowen would have her attractions as well.

'Although Ma's right it does get a bit

lonely at times,' the girl added.

'So perhaps you won't be staying much longer?'

'Well, to be honest we were thinking of leaving. But how could we do so now, with all this trouble going on?' Maybelle said. 'Mrs Dugdale needs us to help her, the poor lady. It wouldn't be right to throw the house into more turmoil by giving in our notice and making them find two other servants. But I guess once this is all over and Gordon's killer caught we will move on. Maybe California after all.'

Meade waited until Mrs Darcy removed the dinner plates and brought them over their pieces of apple pie, before saying, 'How did you get on with Gordon Dugdale?' After all he'd heard of him he wouldn't be surprised to learn that the young man had pestered Katie, seeing it as his right to seduce her, his father's maid.

'He was all right,' Maybelle said with a quick glance at her daughter. She paused as if wondering whether to speak up or not. 'Umm, to tell you the truth we did have a bit of trouble with him at first because he kept hanging around my girl but I had a word with Mr Dugdale and after that Gordon kept his distance and didn't have much to do with either of us. Neither does Miss Ella. She hardly ever speaks to us and she never comes into the kitchen.' She put out a hand to touch Meade's arm. 'Katie's wrong when she says everyone is friendly to us. To Mr and Mrs Dugdale and Miss Ella we're servants not friends. Gordon was the same.' She shrugged. 'That's what we expected really. And at least none of 'em is ever rude or nasty to us and they're all perfectly polite.'

'What about Louis?'

Maybelle's face lit up. 'Oh, Master Louis is a lovely young man, always ready with a pleasant word or two. Completely different from his brother and sister. I feel sorry for him. He always seems lonely.'

Again she glanced at her daughter

and Meade wondered if she harboured hopes that Louis would seek company in Katie's arms. Somehow he couldn't see that going down well with Dugdale.

'Did you see anything on the day Gordon was killed?' he asked. 'Anyone riding out to meet him perhaps?'

'You think the killer is someone at the ranch?' Katie said, her eyes opening wide.

'Maybe.'

'I hope not. That would be frightening.'

'I'm sure you're not in any danger.'

'Oh, it's not that. It's just the thought that someone we know could do something like that is quite awful.'

With a shake of her head Maybelle said, 'Afraid we can't help you, Mr Meade. The kitchen where we spend most of our time is at the back of the house and we can't see any of the actual ranch buildings. We overlook a garden where we grow vegetables and that's where we also have a shed in which we keep our buckboard and the two horses, which are for our use and no one else's. Mr Dugdale said it would be best if we didn't have to go down to the work buildings or mix with the hands. Not that I've got anything against any of 'em. They're nice young men mostly. But it does mean we can come and go as we please and that suits us, don't it, Katie?'

'Yeah, Ma.'

'But that way we don't see much of what is going on and of course the men can't see us.' She smiled. 'Although some do make sure to find an excuse to call in at the kitchen from time to time, don't they, Katie?'

The girl also smiled as she nodded.

'I presume someone knows when you come into town for supplies?'

'Oh, yes. I always tell Mrs Dugdale in case we don't get back in time to make the family their evening meal or to find out if she or Miss Ella wants us to buy anything for them.'

Mrs Darcy brought them over coffee and they were just drinking it when there was a commotion outside.

Two riders galloped sweat-stained horses down the street and pulled to a halt in front of the marshal's office.

'Oh, my goodness,' Maybelle said, a hand going to her heart. 'That's Dick Hoskins. What can he want here in such a hurry?'

'Don't say someone else has been hurt,' Katie added.

12

Closely followed by Maybelle and Katie, who was still limping slightly, Meade hurried out of the café and crossed the road to the marshal's office, urgency in his stride. What the hell was he going to find now? The office was crowded with Cassidy standing up behind his desk faced by the two Broken Spur cowboys, who looked both angry and anxious.

'What's wrong?' Meade demanded.

Hoskins swung round to face him. 'There you are! Louis has disappeared.'

'Oh, no!' Maybelle cried, putting a hand to her mouth in shock, while Katie caught at her other hand and gave a little moan.

'What do you mean?' Meade glanced over at Cassidy, who shrugged slightly as if to say he didn't know what all this meant either. 'How do you know he's disappeared?'

'He rode out this morning to go up to the valley in the hills where the cattle are,' Hoskins explained. 'He was going to talk to Tommy Walker for me and then report back.'

'Morning's not long over, he might still be out in the hills.'

'No, Mr Meade.' Hoskins interrupted impatiently. 'Something is badly wrong. You see, Tommy rode back to the ranch a while ago to tell me he thought the cattle would soon need to be moved to higher ground as the grass was becoming sparse in the meadow. And,' he shook his head, 'not only had Louis not arrived in the meadow but on the way back to the ranch Tommy spotted Louis's riderless horse. There was blood on its saddle.'

'Hell!'

'Exactly.'

'And your man hadn't seen any sign of Louis? Not heard anything?'

Hoskins shook his head again. 'Mind you, Tommy is only a kid and is a bit of a dreamer. For most of the way down through the hills I guess he'd've been thinking about getting back to the ranch and some company and not about much else. Once he found the horse his only thought was to reach help as quickly as possible. As you can imagine, Mr Dugdale is frantic with worry. He took some men out to look for Louis while we came into town to tell you. He wants to know what you're going to do about it.'

As if, Meade thought, it was his fault.

'And it seems to me you're wasting time with all these senseless questions.'

'OK, I'll come back with you now and if necessary we'll set up a proper search party, although perhaps Louis will have been found by the time we get there.'

No one else looked very hopeful about that.

'What about you, Sam?'

'I'll come as well.' Cassidy reached for his Stetson. 'I was going to ride out to see Mrs Bassett, find out if Ralph had been to see her when he said he had, but that can wait. This is more important and you might need all the help you can get.' He also wanted to find out at first hand what was happening in case it affected his town and the people in it.

'Then for God's sake let's get on.' Hoskins was jigging around with impatience.

'We need horses and you'll need fresh animals,' Meade said. 'Or yours will play out before we get halfway to the ranch.'

Hoskins nodded reluctantly to show he realized the truth of this: they'd ridden the animals hard to get here so quickly.

As Meade went to head outside he saw Maybelle and Katie still waiting anxiously by the door.

'We'll start back as well,' Maybelle told him. 'This is a dreadful thing and poor Mrs Dugdale might need our support.'

'Will you be all right travelling on your own?'

'We always have been before.'

'There wasn't a killer out there then.'

'Oh well, oh I don't know ... I certainly don't want any harm coming to Katie.' Maybelle looked concerned and took hold of her daughter's hand. 'And while we've got a rifle neither of us knows much about shooting it.'

'Perhaps you can ride with them,' Meade suggested to the man who'd come into town with Hoskins. 'You'll do more good keeping an eye on them and making sure they're safe rather than coming with us. There's already enough men at the ranch to search for Louis.'

'Good idea,' Hoskins agreed. 'Pete, you OK about that?'

'Sure.' The other man nodded.

'Right now, for God's sake let's go!'

★   ★   ★

Louis blinked open his eyes on to a canopy of green. Where was he? What was he doing lying on the ground, feeling hot, sweaty and uncomfortable? Then with a surge of fright he remembered. He'd been shot. He glanced down at his shirt. It was stiff with sticky blood and more blood was seeping from the wound in his arm. But it was strange, although he remembered feeling pain at the time, now he could hardly feel anything at all.

He couldn't stay where he was. He had to climb back up the hill to the trail. Was the would-be killer still around? No, he must have gone by now, couldn't still be looking for him. Must believe him dead. And he would be dead soon because he probably wouldn't be missed for hours yet and when people did come out looking for him he doubted whether anyone would find him if he remained here.

He tried to get up. And that was when the pain hit him, hard. Shafts of agony ran up and down his arm and chest while his head span and he felt weak and light-headed from the loss of blood.

With a groan he sank back down. He wasn't going anywhere. He was going to die just like Gordy.

★ ★ ★

The Broken Spur ranch was in turmoil.

Everyone, including Mrs Dugdale and Ella, who were both white-faced and hugging one another, had gathered at the corrals, watching and waiting for Meade to arrive. Dugdale was back from his search and was trying to comfort his wife and daughter.

No one quite knew what to do.

Dugdale wasn't used to being so indecisive. Usually he thought out a plan and acted upon it. Now all he could do was wait for the governor's man and hope Meade had something in mind.

It was a tremendous relief for everybody when the three riders were spotted coming along the trail from the hills.

When he, Cassidy and Hoskins dismounted by the worried group of people, Meade saw tears in Celia Dugdale's eyes and she was clinging to her daughter, perhaps scared she wouldn't be able to stand without support, while Dugdale suddenly looked like an old man.

Obviously, Louis was still missing.

Celia took a step towards him and said, 'Please, Mr Meade, you must find my boy. You must. He must be all right. I couldn't bear to lose another child. I can't stand this waiting.'

'It's all right, Ma, don't fret.' Ella drew her mother back into the fold of her arms.

'Did you find anything at all?' Meade asked turning to the rancher.

'No. There was no sign of Louis. Not anywhere.' Dugdale ran a hand over his face. 'We rode up and down the trail, called out to him — ' He broke off unable to go on.

'All right, we'll go out again straightaway,' Meade said. 'Sam and I will go with you and a couple of others along the trail Louis took — '

'He wasn't there!' Dugdale interrupted with an angry snort.

'Sir, he must be somewhere and that's the best place to look for him. But you'd also better send Hoskins and some of the men out into the hills in case Louis has for some reason wandered away from the trail.'

'Yes, all right.'

Meade wasn't sure if the man really agreed with him or whether he simply didn't want to waste time arguing. It didn't matter. They had to get going.

'In the meantime Mrs Dugdale and Ella should go back to the house and stay inside with a couple of your men standing guard.'

Dugdale raised agonized eyes towards him. 'You think they're in danger?'

'It's a chance we can't take.'

'You're right.' The rancher looked as if his world was tumbling down around him. 'God, I've always believed the Broken Spur to be impregnable, somewhere safe for my family, but now . . .' Again his voice faded away.

'I'll sort something out,' Hoskins said.

'You'd better.' Dugdale turned to him, eyes glittering with anger. 'If you hadn't sent Louis so far from the ranch none of this would've happened. You should've found him something to do around the ranch.'

'I'm sorry, sir, I didn't think he would be in any danger.'

'Well he damn well was!'

'I'm sure we'll find Louis and soon.' Meade got in between the two men. 'He can't have gone far.' He tried to sound hopeful and determined but he thought that if Dugdale had already searched the trail and not found any sign of Louis then it was unlikely they would have any luck.

'I hope you're right. What the hell is happening around here? I can't lose both my sons. I just can't. And it would destroy Celia.' It was with a shambling gait that Dugdale went over to his wife and persuaded her and Ella to accompany him to the house. On their way both women looked back at Meade several times.

'They're expecting a lot of you,' Cassidy said. 'Think we'll find Louis?'

'Well he's got to be somewhere. We'll find him eventually but I'm afraid that by the time we do it might be too late for him.'

13

Everyone was eager to get going and so it wasn't long before the men rode out from the Broken Spur. The group led by Hoskins split from the other one to ride up into the hills, leaving Meade, Cassidy, Dugdale and two cowboys, one of whom was Tommy Walker, to follow the trail Louis had taken.

Dugdale rode in front, face grim, mouth set in a thin line, saying nothing, not wanting to speak to anyone.

Cassidy said to Meade, 'He's never faced anything like this before and he can't understand what's going on. Can't understand why all this is happening to his family.'

'Nor can I,' Meade confessed. 'From what I've been told Louis and his brother were completely different characters, did different things. Whoever shot Gordon can have no reason to shoot Louis.' Yet he knew there must be a reason and it was up to him to find out what it was.

'It is a puzzle especially as we don't know for sure that Louis has been shot.'

'He must have been. If he'd just had an accident and fallen off his horse he would've been found on the trail. And don't forget the blood on the saddle.'

'I know.'

'There's another mystery about all this too. Louis told me that Gordon always did the same thing when he went into Sycamore Corner and so the killer would've known he'd be coming back to the ranch the next day. All he had to do was lay in wait for him. But how did the killer know where Louis would be? Dugdale decided his son should do something around the ranch that morning over breakfast but no one could've known that or known what Hoskins would ask Louis to do or where he would send him.'

'In which case the killer must be someone on the ranch.'

141

'Or else he's watching the place.'

'I don't like any of this, Jeremiah.' Cassidy looked very worried. 'If Louis is dead, shot dead I mean, Dugdale will be so maddened with grief and anger he'll refuse to listen to reason. He won't stop to think. I mean if he did he'd realize like us that the murderer couldn't come from Sycamore Corner. As it is he'll want to act, to seek revenge. What's to stop him taking some of his men into town and lynching Ralph Addington?'

'You and me I suppose,' Meade said grimly. 'I hope I can count on you standing by me.'

'That you can.' Cassidy nodded. 'But I ain't sure what the two of us will be able to do against Dugdale and his ranch hands.'

Nor did Meade, not really. 'Are there any townsmen you can rely on to help?'

'I guess so. Tony Vaughan for one. There are others who're always ready to form a posse and while this is completely different one or two of 'em might be willing to take up arms against Dugdale.'

Whether that would be enough Meade didn't know. 'Well, it's a problem we'll have to face if and when we come to it. First, we've got to find Louis.'

Soon the small group was riding up through the hills. Although the wide trail was still light enough the trees and bushes on either side were deep in shadow making it impossible to see what might be there. Everyone began to get fidgety, staring round, hands hovering near the butts of their guns, ready for trouble.

But there was nothing to see, nothing out of the ordinary and Meade began to fear they would be unlucky, that somehow Louis was somewhere else. Maybe, he thought, whoever had shot him had moved him, although that wasn't a comfortable idea, or maybe he wasn't badly hurt but, disorientated, he'd wandered off, although surely he couldn't have gone far.

'We're wasting our damn time,' Dugdale growled. 'I shouldn't have listened to you, Meade. We'd better turn back. He's not here.'

'No, wait, look there!' Cassidy interrupted. His sharp eyes had spotted something on the edge of the trail.

'What is it?' Meade asked.

The two men dismounted and went to investigate.

It was blood!

'Quite a lot of it,' Meade said. 'Quite fresh too.' He turned to Dugdale. 'I reckon this is where Louis was shot.'

'It's near where I found the horse,' Tommy Walker put in.

Dugdale got off his horse to join them, staring up and down the trail. 'Where can he be?'

He certainly wasn't anywhere on the path.

'If he's been able to move it must mean he's only wounded, perhaps hardly hurt at all.' Dugdale was clutching at straws.

Meade took charge.

'You two start to search along the trail on the far side,' he said to the cowboys. 'Carefully too, make sure you don't miss anything. Mr Dugdale, you might like to stay here with the horses.' He didn't want an anxious parent getting in his way and the way he spoke didn't permit any argument, although the rancher didn't look any too pleased. 'Sam, come with me.'

And he plunged into the undergrowth.

'You think he's here . . . watch out!' Cassidy caught hold of the back of Meade's coat to stop him tumbling down the slope of a hill that had suddenly opened up in front of them. 'Down there maybe?'

'Looks like it, Sam, some of the bushes have been trampled and there, see, that bush has been uprooted. Let's go down.'

The two men started slowly down the hill. They hadn't gone very far when they saw the body lying inert on the ground, half hidden by some under-growth.

'It's him!'

Cassidy looked up to where Dugdale remained watching them. 'Sir, we've found Louis.'

Immediately, they heard the man crashing down the hill towards them, careless of his own safety.

Meade quickly pushed some of the undergrowth to one side to get at Louis's body. The young man lay on his back, legs sprawled out in front of him. His eyes were closed and he didn't stir as Meade touched him. His shirt was soaked with blood, although thankfully the bleeding seemed to have stopped.

'Is he alive?' Cassidy asked anxiously.

'Just.'

'Where is he?' Dugdale demanded coming to a halt beside them. 'How . . . oh my God! Louis! He's dead isn't he?' The question was asked in a horrified whisper.

'No, sir, he's still breathing. But he's lost a lot of blood. We must get him back to the ranch as quickly as possible and fetch the doctor to look at him.'

146

'I'll get Walker to ride back and bring the buckboard . . . '

Meade caught at the man's arm. 'There's no time. We'll have to carry him on a horse.'

'But that might start the bleeding again,' Dugdale began to protest.

'I'm sorry, sir, but we leave him here any longer I don't hold out much hope.' Meade thought this was the time for bluntness or Dugdale might, through his not wanting to hurt Louis, actually endanger his son's life.

Luckily, Dugdale made no more objection, he had dealt with enough hurt and wounded men before to know Meade was right. Instead he crouched down by his son, brushing back the lock of hair that had fallen over the boy's face. Meade thought there were tears in the man's eyes for he kept his gaze averted.

Cassidy said, 'Jeremiah, you don't need me to help you with Louis so why don't I start for town right away? I can explain what's happened to Doc Addington and escort him back out here.'

'Good idea,' Meade said. The more time they saved the better.

'Will he come? Knowing it's my son's been shot?' Dugdale stared at the marshal. 'Especially as he might be the one doing the shooting.'

'Ralph is a doctor. Healing people comes first with him, whoever they are.' Cassidy spoke a little angrily, not liking the slur on a townsman. 'He'll do his best.'

'I'm not sure I want him touching my son.'

'There's no choice,' Meade reminded Dugdale. 'Louis is too badly hurt for you or me to tend him.'

The man thought for a moment then nodded reluctantly. 'I'll be watching him all the time, you tell him that.'

'Sam, send the two cowboys down here with a couple of blankets so we can carry Louis up between us.'

'I'll be as quick as I can.' Cassidy started the climb back up the hill.

'Will he be all right?' There was despair in Dugdale's voice.

'I don't know, sir, we can only do our best to save him.'

With the rancher's help Meade managed to pull Louis out into the open by which time the two cowboys had come down to join them. It was difficult but with the help of them and the hindrance of Dugdale, who kept telling them to be careful, they moved Louis on to one of the blankets, covering him with the other. With each man holding the corners of the bottom blanket, using it as a makeshift stretcher, they carried him up the hill. It wasn't easy. It took a superhuman effort. They slipped and slid, almost dropped the stretcher at one point, which earned them all a tongue lashing from Dugdale, and by the time they got to the top, they were sweating profusely, panting with the effort, and Tommy Walker had cut his hand badly on a stone.

When he got his breath back, Meade examined Louis, relieved to see the bleeding hadn't started up again and even more relieved to find that the young man was still breathing, although his breathing was ragged and every now and then he uttered a little moan of pain.

'Let's go,' Dugdale said impatiently, not caring about any of them but only about his son.

He mounted his horse and held out his hands. They lifted Louis's inert body in front of him, wrapping the blankets around him. His father held him close.

That way they headed back down the hill.

And finally reached the ranch house.

14

As they rode up to the house the door opened and Celia Dugdale and Ella ran out. They were followed by the Bowens and the two men who had been standing guard.

Meade was relieved to see they were all right; he had feared the worst in their absence.

'Louis!' Celia shrieked, running towards them her hands outstretched as if she would pick up and carry her son into the house by herself. 'How is he? Oh please tell me he's not dead.'

'Don't fret.' Meade hurried up to her leaving the cowboys to help Dugdale with the young man. 'He's been shot but he's still alive. Sam Cassidy has ridden into town for Ralph Addington. They'll be here soon. Come away now. Let them get him inside and into bed.'

Dugdale lifted Louis up in his arms

and with a weeping Celia being comforted by Ella following on behind, carried him into the house.

'Is there anything we can do?' Maybelle asked Meade.

'If you haven't already done so you can make coffee for everyone. I doubt whether any of the family will feel like eating anything but a hot drink would be welcome. And maybe some soup.'

'A good idea. Come on, Katie, let's do what Mr Meade suggests. And when he gets back you might tell Mr Hoskins that if he needs us to feed the men we can do that too.'

'Good, thanks. I'll let you know if there's anything else.' Meade went after the Dugdales up the stairs and along to Louis's bedroom where he had been laid upon the bed.

Celia stood by his side, wringing her hands.

'Take off his shirt,' Dugdale told his wife. 'We can at least bathe the wounds and make sure they're clean before the doc gets here. Come along, Celia, you've helped more than one cowboy who's been shot or hurt. Now help Louis.'

'Yes, yes, of course.' With something to do for her son the woman seemed a little better, although her eyes kept filling up with tears and her hands trembled.

'I'll ask Mrs Bowen to boil some water,' Ella said and headed for the stairs.

'And tear some sheets up into bandages,' Meade called after her. 'The doctor might have need of them.'

Before long they had done all they could. Louis was undressed, the wounds washed and he was being kept warm beneath several blankets. During it all he hadn't regained consciousness, had at one point seemed to be slipping away, but he'd rallied and was now breathing, shallowly to be sure, but at least he was breathing.

All they could do was stay by his bedside and wait for the doctor.

Thinking the family would be better

off left by themselves, Meade went outside and walked down to the corrals to look for Tommy Walker. He found the young man sitting alone on a bench by the barn. He appeared very dejected.

'Hallo, Tommy, isn't it?' Meade sat down by him.

'Yes, sir. Sir, is Master Louis goin' to be all right?'

'I don't know. I hope so. But, son, Louis getting shot isn't your fault. You shouldn't blame yourself.'

'Mr Dugdale and Mr Hoskins might not see it the same way.'

'How's your hand?'

Tommy held out his hand, the palm of which was cut and grazed. 'It hurts and every time I think it's stopped it starts bleeding again.'

'I'll ask the doctor to look at it after he's seen to Louis. Now, Tommy, tell me what happened. You were on your way back to the ranch and then what?'

'I was comin' to tell Mr Hoskins that I thought the cattle would need moving pretty soon. Then I saw Louis's horse standing there on the trail. That's to say I didn't know Master Louis had been riding it, I mean I recognized it as belonging to the Broken Spur.'

Meade nodded to show he understood. 'What did you do?'

'At first I thought the rider must've fallen off and be lying hurt, although I couldn't see no one along the trail. So I caught up the horse and called out several times to see if anyone answered me but no one did.'

'And you hadn't seen anyone else on the way down? Not heard any shots?'

'No, sir.'

'You didn't spot the blood either?'

'No. The horse was a little way from where that was. But I did find the blood on the saddle.' Tommy gulped. 'I suppose I got scared then because after what happened to Mr Gordy I thought someone else'd been shot and that, well, the shooter might still be around.'

'Perfectly understandable.'

'So I rode on here as fast as I could. It was then I learned that it was Master

Louis who'd been riding the horse. It seemed a bit like a bad dream.' He sighed and added sadly, 'I expect I'll be dismissed for not doing more to find him straight off so he could've been brought back here quicker.'

'Maybe,' Meade agreed.

Dugdale was a harsh employer and would want revenge on all sorts of people if Louis was to die. But he'd have to make sure no one was dismissed until he'd found the killer just in case — Tommy Walker was an unlikely murderer but it wouldn't do to take any chances.

* * *

It was late before Cassidy returned with Ralph Addington.

The doctor must have seen the doubt and anger in Dugdale's eyes because he said quickly, 'I've no quarrel with Louis. I promise to do my best for him.'

'You'd better.' Dugdale spoke ungraciously.

'Where is he?'

'I'll show you.'

Meade turned to Cassidy. 'You'd best go along to the kitchen, get Mrs Bowen to give you coffee and something to eat. You look beat.'

'I am.' Cassidy was moving as if every bone in his body ached. 'I just hope it's worth it and we're not too late.'

'Me too.' Meade could foresee all kinds of trouble otherwise. Neither did he like the idea of a young man like Louis being murdered.

After a while Dugdale came back into the room along with Celia and Ella. 'He doesn't want any of the family present while he doctors Louis.'

'He's my son, I should be with him,' Celia protested.

'No, dear, you sit down.' When Celia went to object Dugdale pulled her down by his side, taking hold of her hands. 'You should rest a little.'

'How can I rest when Louis might be dying?'

'Hush, dear, leave it to Addington.

He knows what he's about. Ella, perhaps you'd get us all some coffee. Meade, he'd like you in there with him.'

Probably so he could confirm Ralph had done all he could if he wasn't successful in saving Louis's life. Meade didn't blame him for that.

In the bedroom Meade stood over by the window, not getting in the way, but ready to help when Ralph needed any fetching or carrying. He also held Louis down while Ralph poked for the deepest bullet which was that embedded in the young man's chest. He was impressed with the way the doctor went about his business, carefully and methodically, not making any fuss. But it all seemed to take a long time and he wondered how the family was coping.

Finally Ralph stood up from bandaging Louis's arm. 'I'm done.' He sighed and wiped some sweat from his forehead. 'It'll be touch and go for quite a while, especially over the next couple of days, but I think, hope, you got to him in the nick of time. Any longer and it would have been too late. He'd have been exposed to the elements too long to survive. As it is,' he shrugged, 'I guess it's now up to God.' He washed his hands then dried them on a piece of sheet and looked at Meade. 'I suppose the same person who killed Gordon shot Louis?'

'It must be.'

'Any idea who?'

'Not yet. Nor why.'

'Well, it wasn't me.'

'Have you got a better alibi this time than last?'

Ralph shrugged again. 'Not really. I've been in my surgery most of the day, making notes about my patients and sorting out what medicines I'll need to order. And before you ask, no one saw me.'

'Pity. But don't worry. For various reasons Sam and I know you're not guilty.'

'Thanks, but I'm not so certain Mr Dugdale feels the same way.'

'I'll explain things to him.' Meade

hoped the man would listen and understand.

At that moment there was a tap on the door and it opened to reveal Gus Dugdale. 'My wife is anxious to know how the boy is. And so am I.'

'I've just finished, sir. I've done all I can.'

'Will he live?' Dugdale asked harshly. He was a blunt man and said what had to be said.

'I can't promise anything for certain.' Ralph paused then said, 'Look, sir, I think he'd be better off in town where I can keep an eye on him. Just for a while until — '

'No! My wife wouldn't want that. She'll want to nurse him herself.'

'It might be safer,' Meade suggested.

Dugdale shook his head and strode to the window and back. 'I must be able to protect my own son. I'll look after him and ensure he's never left alone. He'll be safe enough here indoors.'

Meade hoped he was right and didn't point out that both his sons had been shot on Broken Spur land.

'Anyway the journey might prove too much for him.'

'I wasn't thinking we should leave straightaway.' Ralph sounded as if he thought the man was criticizing his skills as a doctor.

Meade frowned at him. Dugdale had enough on his mind without being concerned about not upsetting other people by what he said.

Dugdale turned to Ralph. 'Stay here the rest of the night. You and Cassidy both.'

'I was about to suggest it so that I can check up on Louis tomorrow. And be here in case there's any crisis.'

'Thanks for all you've done.'

Meade said, 'Ralph, go see Maybelle Bowen. She's got coffee on the go. And perhaps you'd take a look at Tommy Walker. He cut his hand quite badly on a sharp stone.'

'All right. Call me at once if anything changes.' Ralph stifled a yawn and with one last backward glance at his patient he went out, shutting the door behind him.

'Are you sure it's best for your son to stay here, sir?' Meade turned to Dugdale.

'I'm not sure of anything any more. I can't think straight. I know Louis would be nearer a doctor in town but I've men here I trust who can mount a guard on my house and my family. God.' The man ran a hand through his hair. 'I can hardly stand all this. Always in the past I've known who was threatening me and mine and been able to do something about it. Now all I seem to do is jump at shadows.'

From the bed behind them Louis moaned and stirred.

'Son! Louis! It's all right. You're back home.' Dugdale went over to him and stroked his hair.

'Pa.' Louis's voice was croaky and Meade helped him sip a little water.

'You're safe now. You were shot. Did you see who shot you?'

'No,' Louis mumbled. 'But I heard a

noise that frightened me.'

Meade and Dugdale glanced at one another.

'What did you hear?' Meade asked.

'It was a Rebel yell.'

15

'Oh my God!' Dugdale moaned and put his head in his hands.

May, 1864 — Georgia.

Colonel Dugdale held up his arm bringing the group of Unionist cavalrymen to an untidy halt behind him. He could hear them muttering and mumbling amongst themselves. Complaining. Moaning. Not that he blamed them.

They were part of Sherman's army and their orders were to scout the area around the town of Dalton and report their findings back to the general.

Everything had seemed straightforward when they had set out early that morning. The air had been fresh and clean. The task not difficult. They would soon be back in camp.

The good mood hadn't lasted long.

Everything had quickly gone wrong. Now not only was it blisteringly hot it was humid too, making them all breathless, sweaty and exhausted. Even worse, somehow they had gotten turned around and they no longer knew where Sherman was. They had been riding for hours and miles, probably going round in circles, and didn't know where they were either. In the middle of the afternoon they were lost in enemy territory.

The countryside was hilly with plenty of trees and bushes. All providing places where Rebels could be hiding, waiting in ambush for them.

Dugdale didn't like the land, the heat or the noises made by the birds and insects. They were alien to him. The skin on the back of his neck tingled with sweat and apprehension.

Even worse nearly all of his men were strangers to him. They were young, eager for the most part, but inexperienced. They were scared and he wasn't sure if he could rely on them if it came to a fight. He wasn't frightened of dying but he really didn't want to be killed, or captured, not now when surely the War was almost over and the South defeated and he could go home to Celia and his family.

How had they gotten so lost? Well he knew who to blame for that. He scowled at Dennis Shipton as the man rode up by him. It might not exactly be the fault of the mealy-mouthed lieutenant — he wasn't a scout or the one who decided their route — but Dugdale despised the man thinking he had no backbone and so blamed him for everything that went wrong.

'Where the hell are we?' Dugdale snapped.

'I'm not sure, sir,' Shipton confessed reluctantly because he was well aware of what the colonel thought of him. 'But Sherman must be in that direction.' He pointed north.

'I know that dammit! But where exactly? How far?'

What lay between them and the

army? Was any of the enemy about?

Shipton didn't answer because he had no more idea than the colonel.

One thing for sure was that Sherman wouldn't be sending anyone out to search for them when they were the ones meant to be scouting the area. Hell! It looked to Dugdale as if he was about to fail in carrying out his orders. He had spent the war succeeding and now he was riding with the great General Sherman himself he wanted to impress the man, not appear like some sort of idiot who shouldn't even be out with a patrol let alone in charge of it. Frustration and fear of what lay beyond the next hill was making his temper unpredictable.

'Sir, the men are tired and thirsty.' Shipton risked a plea on their behalf not sure that it would be granted.

But Dugdale felt the same. 'We'll rest here awhile,' he decided. At least the trees would provide some sort of shade. He glanced up at the slate-blue sky. They must try to reach Sherman before it started to get dark. 'Thirty minutes, no more, no less.'

'Yes, sir.' Shipton gave what Dugdale thought was a sloppy salute and rode back to the men.

Dugdale dismounted, handed his horse's reins to a private and, taking hold of his canteen of warm water, went over to one of the trees where he sat down, resting his back against the trunk. He took off his hat and wiped his forehead and neck free of sweat.

God! How could anyone live out here? Believe this land was worth fighting and dying for? He could hardly breathe and it was only May. God knew what it would be like in the summer. He had spent the rest of the war in Virginia, never coming this far South before. But he'd been eager to join General Sherman in his push through Georgia, seeing it as possibly the last chance to gain some real glory and see some more action. For he had no doubt that Sherman would succeed in what he'd set out to do and once he'd reached the sea the South would be defeated and have no choice but to surrender.

While in a way Dugdale would be sorry when the War was over, when that happened he could put in hand his plans for the future. He knew that after all this fighting his old life in Maine would prove too dull and restricting to be tolerated. He'd long dreamt of heading west and becoming a rancher. Texas had been the place to go before the fighting started but it was part of the South, had declared war on his country, and he wanted nothing to do with it or its people. It would have to be further west: New Mexico or maybe Arizona.

That was the way forward, the way to become rich and powerful. He'd tasted power in the fighting and he didn't want to give it up.

Exactly half-an-hour later they set out again, heading north, hoping that over the next hill they would see something of Sherman's army, even if it was only a faint glimpse of dust on the horizon.

Instead Sergeant Drake exclaimed, 'There, look, Colonel! Rebs!'

The valley below was wide and open with a stream meandering through it. A road — well, a dusty track really — ran in and out of the trees that followed the line of the water.

Dugdale's heart began to pound with excitement. Making their weary way on foot along the road was a bunch of Confederates. Quickly he counted them: seven.

They were no more than boys, wearing tattered grey uniforms, carrying their weapons as if they were too heavy for them, and they were on their own with no officer, not even a sergeant, to give them orders.

Dugdale's eyes scoured the trees to ensure it wasn't some sort of trap but even as he did so, Drake said, 'Can't see no one else about, Colonel. What shall we do?'

Dugdale didn't pause to consider.

His mood boiled over. Action was the only way to relieve his feelings and those of the men with him.

'Let's get them!'

'But, sir,' Shipton was on his other side, 'they're not posing us any threat. Shouldn't we just let them be on their way?'

Hell! Trust the mealy-mouthed lieutenant to suggest something stupid like that!

'They're the enemy, Lieutenant.' Dugdale's voice was icy cold, unlike the hot pounding of his heart.

'They're just boys.'

'So what? They've got guns. They know how to fire them don't they? Some of the men with us aren't much older. Should we really run the risk of them being shot by those goddamn Johnny Rebs down there just because you're lily-livered and want to let the bastards go? They could pose a threat to General Sherman.'

'That's not likely, sir.'

For answer Dugdale swore at the

man and drew his sword from its scabbard. The others, except for the mealy-mouthed lieutenant, did the same. Anticipation rippled through them all. Here was the chance to defeat the enemy, a chance to show that they weren't really scared, were ready to fight for their country and for each other.

'Charge!'

They broke into a gallop. And were halfway down the hill before the Confederates realized they were coming.

The Rebels swung round and seeing the danger they were in, with no one to lead them, started to cry out and run, to scatter in all directions.

Dugdale smiled in triumph. His mouth was open and he thought he was yelling, although he wondered if he was in fact making any sound. He was in the lead as the horses hit the valley floor, his men close behind, and raising his sword he rode towards the enemy.

From somewhere close behind him he heard the sound of a shot. The Rebel nearest him stopped suddenly and threw up his arms. Before he could fall he was shot again and the force of the bullet sent him tumbling sideways into the stream where he lay face down in the water.

The next two boys caught at one another and stopped. Kneeling down on the ground they threw away their weapons and raised their arms. They were shivering with fright.

'They're surrendering, sir!' Shipton yelled in Dugdale's ear. 'Stop this! They're giving up!'

'Shut up, you stupid bastard!'

'Sir, no!'

Shipton grabbed for the reins of Dugdale's horse and pulled hard. The horse whinnied and it was with some difficulty that Dugdale stayed in the saddle. Instead to his glee it was Shipton who was jerked off the back of his own animal to land in the dusty earth. Somehow the lieutenant managed to retain his hold on the reins, even though he cried out in pain, and dragged the horse to a halt, again nearly unseating the colonel.

'Get out of my damn way!' Dugdale yelled and raised his sword.

Shipton ducked. Dugdale resisted the urge to bring the weapon down on the man's head.

'This is wrong.'

'Let go!' Dugdale kicked his heels into his horse's sides and urged it forward.

The horse responded and Shipton was forced to let go or be dragged along the ground. He fell over and could do nothing more to stop his commanding officer.

Laughing, Dugdale bore down on the nearest Rebel. He was aware of a white face, terrified eyes staring at him, mouth agape. He wielded the sword. Its point struck home. The boy collapsed, screaming, then screaming again before falling quiet. Another Confederate had taken to his heels but he was mown down by a couple of cavalrymen, their horses riding right over him.

A couple of others had started a futile resistance and one of the Unionists was knocked from his saddle, which in Dugdale's heated mind completely justified the action.

All around came the sound of shots, of cheers, yells and the terrified cries of frightened, dying men. The squealing of a wounded horse.

Suddenly the last Confederate, his hands in the air, was shot several times. He was jerked backwards and after he fell he lay still.

It was over.

All at once it was deathly quiet except for the screams of one young man. They were quickly silenced with a gunshot.

The earth seemed to be dyed red. The stream ran with blood. Along with one Northerner the seven Confederates were dead. A couple lay along the road, one was under the trees. The rest were in the water.

Shipton ran up and came to a halt staring at the scene in appalled horror.

His uniform was covered with dust, he'd lost his hat and Dugdale had time to think that it was the first time he'd seen the mealy-mouthed lieutenant look untidy and dirty.

There were tears in the man's eyes. 'Oh my God, sir, what the hell have you allowed to be done?'

16

'They called it The Atrocity,' Dugdale said.

Meade was inclined to do the same.

The two men were in Dugdale's study and now the rancher paused in his story to pour them out more whiskey. The room was lit by two oil lamps and the rest of the house was very quiet. Dugdale ran a hand over his face, looking ashen and exhausted.

'What happened?' Meade asked, his voice sounding harsh to his ears.

He wasn't about to waste time feeling sorry for the rancher. When he'd been a lawman he'd known times when it was impossible not to shoot at someone — and kill, too — but surely, whatever the circumstances, to use superior numbers to kill seven scared boys, even if they wore an enemy uniform, and who were surrendering, was completely and utterly wrong. Could never be justified or explained away by saying it was war and that bad things took place in war.

At least Dugdale hadn't tried to excuse it as anything other than the fact that their bloodlust was up for no real good reason and he'd allowed his men to kill indiscriminately; had led them in what was done. Even now, after all this time, he didn't seem to be sorry or believe what he'd done to be wrong.

Except that now the ghosts of the past were surely here in the present.

'We got back to Sherman's camp early the next morning,' Dugdale went on. 'The mealy-mouthed lieutenant went to him straight off and reported me. Trust that bastard. I was arrested and held for court martial. But, Meade, this was the last days of the War. Sherman wanted to march on Atlanta. All the talk was of defeating the South at last. There was already an air of jubilation about the whole Union army. Who cared about seven Johnny Rebs?'

Obviously not Dugdale.

Probably not Sherman either. So many men, so many other boys, had died in the conflict and the general was only concerned about bringing it all to an end.

'The trial was held quickly and I was acquitted. I returned to my unit for the last glorious days of victory. I never saw the mealy-mouthed lieutenant again, God knows where he went, but it was a good job he went somewhere. Because I don't know how I'd've behaved towards him if I had met him again and he certainly wasn't any too popular with any of my men. They considered me a hero.' Dugdale sat back with something like satisfaction in his face and voice.

Angry with him because of the senseless killing then and the senseless killing now because of it, Meade thought it was time to take the man down a peg or two. Making no secret of his anger he said, 'But someone involved in that atrocity is responsible for killing Gordon and shooting Louis.'

179

'Yes.'

For a moment Meade almost allowed himself to feel sorry for Dugdale. The man's past was coming back to haunt him in the worst possible way. He certainly felt sorry for his two sons who had been too young to have had anything to do with the War. What had happened wasn't their fault but now one was dead and the other possibly dying. Their mother and sister, also innocent bystanders, were suffering too.

'Have you any idea who it could be who's out for revenge?'

'No, of course not!' Dugdale snapped. 'This is all as much a surprise to me as it is to you. And at the moment I can't think straight.' Then he sighed and downed his whiskey in one gulp, pouring himself out more. 'No,' he went on. 'I've hardly thought about the event' — no need for Meade to know about his nightmares — 'in the last fifteen years. It never occurred to me that that might be behind Gordy's killing.' He sighed again. 'It never once crossed my mind that anyone

180

would come after me to seek vengeance. Especially after all this time.'

'No, it does seem a long while to wait,' Meade agreed. 'Although there could be a good reason for that.'

'Such as?'

'Such as a youngster growing up and learning the fate of a relative. Maybe it's someone who's been ill or in prison.' Dugdale didn't look impressed at such reasoning so Meade went on, 'Or even simply the fact that it's taken this long to trace your whereabouts. America is a vast country and knowing you fought for the North a person might have searched for you there first.'

'That's possible.' Dugdale nodded. 'I mean my name and where I lived would've been known to anyone who cared to look because of the court martial. But I left Maine and moved out here almost as soon as the War was over. And back then there were no newspapers, no telegraph, no way of communicating with the East let alone the South. But it wouldn't be so difficult to discover my whereabouts these days when we're more civilized, especially as I'm well known and my name appears in the papers quite often.'

'Whoever it is, whatever the reason for the delay you've been found.'

A look almost of panic crossed the rancher's face. 'Hell, it could be anyone.'

'That it could.'

'One thing is for sure it's no one on the Broken Spur. I refuse to employ Rebs. But it could be someone employed on a neighbouring ranch. Their owners aren't as particular as me. I don't think there are any Rebs in Sycamore Corner.' His tone seemed to imply that he'd have made it so tough on them they wouldn't stay long; perhaps had done so in the past.

'Evidently there was a Southerner in the Sycamore Stop the day before Gordon was shot. They were playing cards.'

Dugdale slammed his hands down on

the desk almost knocking his glass over. 'That's your damn answer then! I wish you or Cassidy had told me this before. You're both just wasting my time. He's the one responsible.'

'Not necessarily,' Meade warned. 'But he certainly bears looking into.'

'I'll send men into town to arrest him and bring him back here.' Dugdale half rose from his seat. 'Then I'll see to it he don't cause me or anyone else any more grief.'

'No, you won't. If anyone is going to arrest him it'll be me or the marshal and that only when I know he's guilty and I've got the evidence to convict him.' Meade was worried that Dugdale would still send men galloping into town and once there they could cause trouble when they didn't find their quarry. He had to stop that before it started. 'Besides he's not in Sycamore Corner any more.'

'Then where the hell is he?'

But Meade had no intention of telling Dugdale that. He didn't want

Piers Laidlaw to be the victim of a lynch mob.

'I want him found and questioned. You understand me?'

Meade didn't like being given orders so he said nothing in reply.

'There is another possibility,' Dugdale went on after he'd had another glass of whiskey and calmed down somewhat.

'Oh, who?'

'The mealy-mouthed lieutenant, Dennis Shipton. He didn't like or approve of me and I was none too fond of him either. He was out to get me and he believed the court martial would convict me and I'd end up in prison or maybe even in front of a firing squad. Instead I was acquitted and all it did was make him look bad and become even more unpopular than he was before.'

'Do you know where he went?'

'No, after the court martial he was sent elsewhere.'

'Was he a career soldier?'

'Not as far as I was aware. I didn't know much about him. Or want to know either. Except that he was a thorn in my side.'

'Then why should he bother to seek revenge on you? All right, he was angry over killing those boys but none of them meant anything to him personally. And the fact that he looked bad couldn't have mattered once he left the army when the War was over and the War was over within a very short while.'

'Perhaps you're right.' Dugdale was obviously reluctant to give up on the idea.

'Besides, why would he use a Rebel yell? Surely that must indicate that the killer is a Southerner.'

'Yeah, I guess so. No, it must be this bastard who was in town. He's the one and I want him stopped.' Dugdale put his head in his hands for a moment then looked up at the other man. 'Christ, Meade, have you ever heard it? The Rebel yell I mean.'

'No.'

'It's enough to send shivers down your spine. Once heard it's never forgotten.'

★　★　★

Later Meade sat with Sam Cassidy out on the veranda, drinking coffee. Although Ralph Addington was in bed, neither of them could sleep. It was still dark although there was a faint light of dawn in the eastern sky. Every so often the guards patrolling round the house called out to one another but otherwise it was quiet except for once the yip of a coyote came from close by.

Meade said, 'I know I mentioned Laidlaw to Dugdale simply because he's from the South and happened to be around at the time of Gordon's murder but I don't think he's guilty, although I've got to make sure one way or the other.'

'The fact that he was meant to have arrived in town by chance could be false,' Cassidy pointed out. 'He could've come there with purpose in mind.'

'I still believe it's more likely to be a ranch hand.'

'Why?'

'Both Gordon and Louis were shot near the ranch not near the town. Like we said earlier, the killer knew their movements.'

'But as we've also said, someone could be out there somewhere.' Cassidy indicated the desert stretching all round them. 'Watching and waiting for his chance. And that someone could be Laidlaw.'

'In which case it'll be nigh on impossible to find him. Hoskins and his men searched and failed. I might get them to go out again though. Give them something to occupy their time.'

Cassidy paused to finish his coffee. 'What are you going to do next?'

'I'll ride back to town with you and Ralph.'

'Don't you think one of us should stay out on the ranch?'

'Yes, I do, but I don't see that it's possible. I'll have to ride to Leeville and hope this Laidlaw is still there. Ralph has his patients to look after and you've got the town to police. Besides,

Dugdale has enough men out here that he can trust to set a guard on his family. I'm hoping the killer won't try anything more while everyone is alert and ready.'

'Don't forget the killer has shown himself to be quick and clever. Determined too. He could find the chance to slip by the guards.'

'I know but I don't see what else I can do.' Meade sighed. He certainly couldn't be in two places at once and he couldn't expect Sam to neglect Sycamore Corner whose citizens paid his wages, nor Ralph to neglect his surgery. And while he believed that riding after Laidlaw would probably prove to be a wild goose chase it was something that had to be done.

★　★　★

How could Louis Dugdale not be dead? He'd been shot three times. He should be dead.

And now because Louis had heard the Rebel yell, Dugdale knew all this was happening because of The Atrocity. It would have been better for him to puzzle over the wheres and whys for a while longer. Still that couldn't be helped. It just meant more care and cunning would have to be taken. No one, not even that clever bastard, Mr Meade, was going to get in the way. And as he, given the chance, might figure out the truth it was best if he was never given the chance.

17

Meade looked round the table at the subdued and bone-weary group of people who were eating the breakfast prepared by Maybelle Bowen and served by Katie.

Neither Dugdale nor Ella looked as if they had slept. Celia wasn't present. She insisted on staying in Louis's bedroom, sitting by his side, in case when he woke up he wouldn't know where he was or what had happened. Or in case he suddenly worsened and she needed to call for help, although no one mentioned that.

Hoskins had arranged the men so that as well as getting on with the work on the ranch they could all take turns at guard duty. Now a cowboy sat outside Louis's room while others patrolled the ranch headquarters. Meade hoped it would be enough. At least everyone was alert and ready to tackle any trouble.

As Ralph Addington came into the room, Dugdale looked up anxiously. 'How is he?'

Ralph sat down opposite Ella and smiled. 'Louis is still unconscious but there's been no more bleeding and thankfully there's no sign of a fever. He's asleep and resting comfortably. In fact sleep will be the best cure for him. I think he'll recover.'

'Thank God!' Ella exclaimed, smiling back at the young man. 'What good news!'

'I can't promise anything,' Ralph added in warning. 'It's still early days but I'm hopeful.'

Dugdale turned to his daughter. 'Ella, now you've finished breakfast you should go and sit with Louis and let your mother have a rest. She's been with him all night.'

For a moment Meade thought that Ella didn't look all that pleased at the order. He wondered if her professed worry about Louis was more concern for herself, in case she was in danger, rather than concern for her brother, and that her relief at his surviving the night was really so she could flirt with Ralph. Perhaps he was being unfair. After all Louis *was* her brother and she had already lost Gordon. And her whole way of life had been thrown into turmoil.

Anyway she said, 'Of course, Dad, I'll go now.'

'Call me if there's any change.'

'I will.' The girl stood up. 'Thank you, Mr Meade, for finding my brother when you did and thank you, doctor, for helping him. We're all in your debt.'

Meade nodded and hid a smile as Ralph blushed furiously. The young man was obviously smitten. He just hoped Ralph's heart wasn't going to be broken again as it had been with Polly Murdock but he had a feeling it would be. So did Cassidy if his scowl was anything to go by. Ella was the type of girl to flirt with every man she met. Perhaps she had even flirted with Sam, although he was surely too down to earth and sensible to be fooled into thinking it meant anything more.

Well, Ralph's heart was nothing to do with him and it surely wouldn't be long before he met a suitable girl, especially as he had a good deal to offer.

'As soon as Ralph has had something to eat we must be on our way.'

'Yes, Meade, I suppose you must.' Dugdale sounded disappointed. 'I wish you could stay here.'

'You'll be OK with your men to keep watch. It's more important I try to find the killer and stop him.'

Dugdale nodded. 'You're right of course.'

'And you must send into town at once if you need me,' Ralph added.

'Yes — '

All hell seemed to break loose.

There were screams followed at once by a loud whooshing noise from somewhere at the rear of the house. Then came an enormous bang. More screams and yells. To which both

Cassidy and Ralph added startled exclamations.

'What the hell was that?' Dugdale cried.

'Quick!' Meade pushed his chair back with such force it fell over and with the other three men close on his heels he rushed from the room. 'It sounded like it came from the kitchen.'

In the hallway they heard Celia calling out from Louis's room and they saw Ella picking herself up from where the explosion had knocked her over.

'Are you all right?' Ralph turned to help her.

'Yes. What's wrong?' She was shaking.

'Go to your mother,' Dugdale ordered her. 'Stay with her and Louis. You,' he yelled at the cowboy who had appeared at the top of the stairwell, 'stay close by them.'

'Keep your eyes open!' Meade called to him.

Another scream echoed round them as they raced down the hall.

Katie, Meade thought, or maybe her mother.

'Sam.' He caught hold of the younger man's arm. 'Go outside. Get round to the kitchen that way. Ralph, go with him. And watch yourselves. There could be a shooter out there.'

He feared they could all be heading into some sort of trap and didn't want them all arriving in the same place and at the same time.

Dugdale was in front of Meade and he reached the kitchen first. He flung open the door before Meade could stop him or warn him.

Onto a scene of chaos.

A fire was burning out of control on the range. Flames licked at the walls and curtains. A young cowboy was attempting to tear the curtains down and not having much success in his panic. The kitchen door was open and outside Maybelle was bent over Katie, who lay on the ground. A cowboy stood guard over them both, revolver out and ready.

'We ain't seen anyone,' Cassidy said as he and Ralph appeared at a run from round the corner of the house. 'My God, what's happened?'

'Ralph, see to Miss Bowen, make sure she's not hurt.' Meade took charge. 'You,' he said to the cowboy in the kitchen, 'get Hoskins.'

But there was no need for that because more men were already arriving from the direction of the work buildings, the foreman in the lead. He was relieved. Hoskins was a good, capable man who wouldn't need Meade's help to order the hands about or to know what to do.

'Mr Dugdale, go up to your wife. Tell her there's a fire in the kitchen but it'll soon be under control.'

As the man hesitated Meade gave him a push. He didn't seem to like that but nevertheless did as he was told, shutting the door behind him so the flames didn't have a chance to spread.

Already Meade was pulling at the curtains, tearing them, dragging them away from the windows. With them he tried to smother the fire but it had gained too much of a hold.

'Jeremiah, come on out of there,' Cassidy called, afraid the man would be hurt. 'Wait for the others with water. They'll be here in a minute or two.'

Meade realized the marshal was right. Wheezing from breathing the smoke he went outside where Hoskins had young men running this way and that, collecting pails and buckets, setting up a line. It seemed to be all confusion but it soon sorted itself out.

'Maybelle, what happened?'

The cook looked up at Meade with tears in her eyes. 'I don't rightly know, sir. The fire in the range suddenly flared up with a tremendous bang for no reason at all. The force of it knocked Katie off her feet. Then everything started to burn and there was suddenly so much smoke I couldn't see properly. My only thought was for my little girl and I opened the door and managed to drag her outside.'

'Is she all right?' Meade turned to Ralph.

The doctor looked up from where he was examining the girl. 'I think her falling over probably got her out of the way of the flames and so saved her from suffering any burns. But she is shocked and bruised.'

'It happened so quickly,' Katie mumbled. 'There was nothing we could do to stop it.'

'You're safe now.' Ralph patted her arm.

Twisting her hands together Maybelle went on, 'I thought we would be trapped and burnt alive.'

Cassidy surveyed the kitchen. 'I don't think you were in that much danger.'

'I don't see how you can say that when you weren't there. It was so frightening and I didn't know what to do.' Maybelle shot the marshal a look of dislike. 'Luckily two of the men were close by and they came to help us. Oh dear, no one's been hurt have they? The fire won't spread will it?'

'No.' Meade saw that Hoskins had got the line of men working quickly and efficiently. Already the fire was almost out. Smoke rose into the air where there had been flames. 'Everything is under control.'

'Thank God.'

Obviously unable to keep away, even for the sake of his wife, Dugdale came hurrying round the side of the house. 'How is everyone? My God, Mrs Bowen, your daughter isn't injured, is she?'

'Not badly, no sir. Thank you for asking.'

'It's all right now,' Meade reassured the man. 'The fire is more or less out.'

'But what caused it in the first place?' Dugdale looked as if he couldn't take any of it in.

'Sir, sir.' Hoskins emerged from the kitchen holding a bundle of blackened scraps of rags. 'Sir, I found these stuffed down into the range. And, sir, they've been doused in oil. When the fire hit them that's what caused everything to go up with a bang.'

Dugdale groaned and ran a hand over his face. 'It was deliberate then?' He had obviously been hoping against hope for it to have been an accident.

'Looks that way,' Hoskins said and looked at Meade who nodded. Neither man could see how to explain it otherwise.

'Katie and me could both have been killed.' Maybelle started to cry. 'Oh, Mr Dugdale, sir, who's doing all these dreadful things? Why should they want to hurt us?'

'It's not you they want to hurt but me and my family. You just happened to be in the way.' The rancher sounded close to despair.

'Mr Meade.' Katie spoke from where she still sat on the ground, leaning back against Ralph. She coughed as if her throat hurt her.

Meade hunkered down in front of her. 'What is it?'

'I was looking out of the window earlier this morning while Ma was getting breakfast ready. I saw a man riding off in that direction.' She pointed away from the ranch towards the low hills in the distance.

'There ain't no cattle over there,' Hoskins put in, sounding puzzled. 'One of my men wouldn't've had any reason to ride that way. And there ain't no other ranches nearby either.'

'Did you recognize him?' Meade asked.

'No.' Katie shook her head. 'He was too far away. And then he disappeared over the horizon.'

'D'you think it could be our killer?' Cassidy said as Meade stood up. His eyes raked the horizon. 'Can't see no one now.' He pulled the other man a little way away from the others so they wouldn't hear what he had to say. 'And, Jeremiah, there's a trail through the hills that leads to Leeville.'

'So it could have been Laidlaw?'

'Yeah.'

'For God's sake don't say anything to Dugdale. I don't want him doing something stupid.'

'I won't. What I can't understand is how this was done when the men were out guarding the house.'

'Me neither, but I intend to find out.' Meade stared at the hills. 'I'd better go take a look in case the bastard is still hanging around.'

'I'll come with you.'

'No, Sam, you stop here for a while and make sure everything really is OK. And that the Dugdales are reassured we're doing our best for them. If I don't find the rider I'll see if I can discover any tracks to follow. Even if I don't I'll ride on into Leeville. Discover if Laidlaw is still there and what he has to say for himself. Meanwhile you go on back to Sycamore Corner with Ralph and I'll join you there as soon as I can.'

'If you're sure?'

'I am. Anyway there's something I need you to do.'

'What?'

'When you get back I want you to telegraph the governor's office and ask them if they can find out anything about Dugdale's court martial. It took place in Georgia in May, 1864. Especially ask if they can discover the names of the Confederates who were killed. Also if anything is known about the whereabouts of Lieutenant Dennis Shipton. I think he'd been with Dugdale for quite a while but I don't know anything else about him.'

'OK.'

18

Cassidy waited while Meade saddled up his horse then watched him ride away before walking back to the house. The fire was out and a couple of the men were clearing things out of the kitchen. Katie and her mother stood nearby watching them, as did Dugdale, Hoskins and Ralph.

Dugdale was in a towering rage, with red spots on his ashen cheeks and his hands clenched by his sides.

His anger was made worse because he was also scared and didn't know what to do. He had fought Southerners in the War then Apaches and outlaws out here in Arizona. But they were enemies he'd been able to see. Now he was facing an unknown and invisible adversary. A foe who was out to punish him and his family for what he'd done all those years ago. A foe who was clever enough that so far he'd avoided being identified and caught. Someone who would stop at nothing, and hurt anyone who got in his way so as to achieve his purpose.

With glittering eyes, he swung round to face Hoskins. 'I thought your men were meant to be guarding the ranch! They didn't do much of a job! Where the hell were they? How come someone was able to get past them, get in the house and stuff oil-soaked rags on the range? Hell, we could all have been blown up with it or burnt to death!'

Hoskins looked as if he wished he was elsewhere. In defence of the cowboys he said, 'It was night. The men can't be everywhere at once. It would be quite easy for someone determined enough to slip by them.'

'And then get in the house?' asked Cassidy who was listening. He sounded doubtful. 'Did anyone notice whether one of the doors or windows was broken this morning?' His gaze swept over Dugdale, the Bowens and Ralph.

Who all shook their heads.

'Of course we didn't because nothing was,' Dugdale said in a scornful tone. 'Surely we'd've heard something like breaking glass. None of us was sleeping much if you remember. And I made certain the windows and doors were locked tight last night.'

'I've looked round the outside of the house, Marshal, and haven't spotted a break-in,' Hoskins added.

'Mrs Bowen.' Dugdale swung round to the woman so fast she took a startled step backwards. 'I hope you locked up properly last night. Didn't leave the kitchen door or window open?'

'No, I never!' Maybelle was shocked. 'I'm always careful and I was especially careful in the circumstances. Everything was just as Katie and I left it when we went into the kitchen this morning.'

'Well, Cassidy is right, somehow someone must have gotten in during the night, unless — ' Dugdale came to a halt and stared angrily at Ralph. 'Unless it was an inside job and the goddamned bastard was already in the house. It was you, wasn't it? I knew it. You're the goddamned killer!' He raised an arm and Katie gave a frightened squeak.

Quickly Cassidy stepped in front of Ralph.

'No,' Ralph protested his innocence.

'If Ralph was the killer why would he have done his best for Louis?' Cassidy said, his hand hovering over the butt of his gun for Dugdale looked murderous, quite ready to gun down even an unarmed man. 'He could easily have said it was too late to help him and let him die. And Ralph isn't from the South.'

The doctor looked puzzled at that statement.

'So he says.'

'No, I come from New York. What's this all about?'

Neither Cassidy nor Dugdale answered him.

'Nor is he stupid. If by chance he was the killer — '

'Which I'm not!'

' — he wouldn't do something that would immediately point to him.'

'I haven't done anything.'

'Sir,' Cassidy said, 'let Mr Meade sort this out for you. He's doing his best and he's near to making an arrest.' He didn't think Jeremiah would mind him lying.

'Yes, sir,' Hoskins put a hand on his boss's arm, 'don't do nothing rash.'

Slowly, reluctantly Dugdale relaxed his belligerent stance and everyone breathed sighs of relief. 'All right but just remember I'm keeping an eye on you all. Hoskins, take a good look round, make sure the doors and windows are secure. I don't want the killer getting in for a second time. And tell the men that if I catch any of 'em slacking they're dismissed.'

'Yes, sir.' Hoskins was obviously glad to get away from his boss's temper and the blame that seemed to be laid at his door.

Dugdale called after him, 'If they see anyone tell 'em to shoot to kill.'

Cassidy opened his mouth to object before realizing that he had no authority here and that the rancher was unlikely to take any notice of him. And who could blame him for wanting to protect his family?

He glanced up at the window which was that of Louis's bedroom. Ella stood there, looking out, appearing quite forlorn and alone and not at all like her usual vivacious self. She must be wondering if her life would ever return to normal: privilege and money meant nothing now in the face of danger and turmoil.

'Ralph, you'd better go and see how Louis is and then we can leave for town.'

'All right, Sam.' The young man looked worried. 'I don't like leaving him. Perhaps one of us should stay here.'

'I've got things to do for Jeremiah in town. And you've got your patients to look after.'

'I suppose so,' Ralph agreed reluctantly.

'And it probably ain't a good idea for you to be here alone with Dugdale, especially with the mood he's in.'

'No, you're right. OK, I won't be long.'

Left to himself, Cassidy stood by the kitchen door taking in the scene. He frowned. There was something wrong about all this but he couldn't figure out what it was. Something that had been said or done. He wished he could think of what it was and he wished too that Meade was still here so he could talk it over with him. Should he speak to Ralph about his worries? But he decided not to, thinking that Jeremiah wouldn't approve of him doing so with anyone other than him.

He'd just have to wait until he saw the governor's man again and he wondered how he was getting on. Maybe, hopefully, he would find evidence to convict Piers Laidlaw of the crime and the matter could be laid to rest.

★ ★ ★

So that idiot Cassidy was not quite the buffoon he had always appeared. He'd obviously sensed something was wrong. He was another one proving difficult. Well, he could be dealt with in the same way as anyone else who tried to interfere in plans long made for the downfall of Colonel Gus Dugdale. No one was going to stop them from being carried out.

19

Meade reached the first of the foothills without seeing anyone. But then he hadn't really expected to. The rider Katie spotted earlier had a good lead on him and wouldn't hang around once the fire had started. He was probably miles away by now. Neither did he find any fresh tracks. Even so each time he crossed a ridge he brought the mare to a halt and scanned the land in front of him and he kept his rifle out and laid across his saddle horn and kept his eyes peeled as well.

He soon realized that whoever he was following could have ridden off in any number of directions. He needed that ex-army tracker who was with the sheriff chasing Apaches and who might be able to find sign that eluded him.

It was very quiet in the pine-clad hills, cool too, so despite all his precautions he made good time, reaching Leeville at just gone noon. It was a tiny place nestled at the end of a long narrow valley: just one short street with a store, a café, marshal's office and a saloon, surrounded by twenty or so houses. It catered to the nearby ranchers and farmers who, if they wanted anything more than necessities, had to make the journey into Sycamore Corner.

Several old-timers sitting round a well watched him as he rode down the street. A few men and fewer women were going in and out of the store and the café. Some stopped to look at him as well. A couple of young cowboys stood drinking in the entrance to the saloon. That was all. It wasn't exactly buzzing.

Meade dismounted in front of the marshal's office, which was nothing but a wooden shack. He stretched wearily, wondering if he was getting too old for all this riding around. At moments like this a career in politics, sitting in a comfortable office, began to look attractive, although he wasn't really sure how he would get on being indoors all day handling paperwork. It wasn't something he really wanted to do right now, but maybe in the future he'd give it consideration.

Luckily, the marshal was at his desk. He was an elderly, plump man with sparse brown hair and a wispy moustache, who looked quite surprised to see his visitor, obviously puzzled what a stranger wanted with him.

Meade introduced himself.

'Dave Freeman.' The man stood up, wiped his hand on his trouser-leg and held it out for Meade to shake. 'What can I do for you?'

Quickly, not going into too many details, Meade explained. 'Do you happen to know if this Southerner, Piers Laidlaw, has been in town and more importantly whether he's still here?'

Freeman nodded. 'He's surely been here, oh last week or so. Been gambling in the saloon and sleeping over there too. Can't say I hold much with gamblers but he seems honest enough and ain't caused no trouble. As to whether he's still in town,' he scratched his chin, 'he certainly was last night when I called in for a drink and no one's said nothing about him moving on. Although I expect he will soon. Ain't much to keep him here.'

'Shall we go and find out?'

'Sure thing, sir.' Freeman jammed a hat on his head and led the way outside. 'We heard about the murder of Gordy Dugdale and now you say t'other Dugdale boy's been shot?'

'That's right.'

'But he's holding his own you say?'

'At the moment.'

'Well, I guess there are quite a few people around here who don't like the Dugdales much. Some've got a grudge goin' against Gus Dugdale, who I hear can be overbearing. I dunno him personally. If he's ever been to Leeville he ain't called on me.' The man chuckled. 'But whether anyone'd resort to killing his kin over his attitude . . . ' He shrugged. 'Here we are.'

The saloon, another wooden hut, was a one-storey building with a falsefront. Another building stood close by at the back which was presumably where Laidlaw had a room and where any prostitutes the place employed satisfied their clients. Inside were no refinements. Just an earthen floor, plain walls and a bar that was a plank of wood resting on empty barrels. This time of day there were only a few people inside. The cowboys who had been in the doorway now lounged by the bar, another cowboy sat at a table with a girl wearing an extremely low-cut dress, and another man sat by himself dealing out solitaire.

'That's him.'

Meade stared. Piers Laidlaw was about forty. Whatever colour hair he'd once had it was now white, although his beard was still brown. He had blue eyes.

'Get you a drink?' Freeman asked.

'Thanks, I'll have a beer.'

Laidlaw looked up at the approach of the two men and in a pronounced drawl said, 'What can I do for you gentlemen? Guess you're not here for a game of chance.'

Meade pulled out a seat opposite the man and sat down, placing his arms on the table. Freeman hovered behind him, seeming more interested in looking at the girl's breasts than listening to any conversation between the two men.

'Name's Jeremiah Meade. I'm from the governor's office in Prescott and I'm here investigating the murder of Gordon Dugdale and the shooting of his brother, Louis.' Meade took a sip of the beer which somewhat to his surprise was cold and clear.

'Oh, really?' Laidlaw scooped up the cards and started to shuffle them in a very professional manner. 'And so you've ridden all this way to talk to me.'

'That's right. Got a few questions for you.'

'May I ask you a question first? What

do you think I have to do with any of it?'

Meade didn't answer but said instead, 'You know what's been happening?'

'Like most everyone else in Leeville I heard about Gordon Dugdale. That was all the talk was about for a while. Can't say I was surprised. The way he acted it was a wonder he hadn't been shot long since. I didn't know about his brother. I didn't know he had a brother. In fact I don't know anything about the family except that evidently none of them likes Southerners.' Laidlaw laughed slightly. 'Even though the War has been over a long time. You would think they could forget and forgive.' He started to lay out the cards in another game of solitaire, concentrating on them rather than on Meade.

'You fought in the War?'

'Yes, sir. I am from Virginia after all and was fighting for my country against the oppression of the North.'

'Not Georgia?'

'No, sir, Virginia. Near Richmond. I

had the honour of serving with General Robert E Lee and was with him from almost the beginning to the sorry end at Appomattox. When I returned home there was little of it left and so I took up the profession of gambler. I'm quite good at it too. What's your interest in where I'm from?'

'I have reason to believe that whoever is behind all this trouble is doing so in revenge for the massacre of some young Confederates that occurred in Georgia during the last days of the War.'

'A massacre?' Laidlaw's eyes narrowed. Sounding angry he went on, 'A lot of wrong was done in Georgia.'

'I know. I don't condone it.'

'But the Dugdale boys must have been too young to be involved.'

'It was the father.'

'Ah! And you think I'm responsible.' Laidlaw began to move the cards about quickly, almost automatically.

'You are from the South . . . '

'Not Georgia.'

' . . . and you were in the vicinity of

the ranch at the appropriate time. You had a run in with Gordon. You left Sycamore Corner early the next day and could have lain in wait for him.'

'Maybe I could but I didn't. I rode straight here to Leeville.'

'Can you prove that?'

'No.'

'So I've only your word for it.'

'Yes.'

'You're still here and could have shot his brother.'

'When was that?'

When had that happened? Meade had to think for a moment. He was surprised that it was only the day before when it seemed so much longer ago. 'Yesterday morning.'

'Then I'm innocent of that and can prove it because I've been here in this delightful saloon ever since I arrived from Sycamore Corner. Playing cards. Practising shuffling and dealing. Making friends with a couple of the girls.' He looked at the prostitute who smiled broadly at him.

'You haven't left Leeville at all?'

'Oh, I might have taken a ride now and then but I haven't been away all that long a time and someone's always accompanied me.' Another glance at the girl. 'I was certainly here all day yesterday. Agnes can vouch for me and so I believe can some cowboys I won a deal of money from at poker, although as they were rather annoyed at losing their grubstake they might not want to alibi me.'

'You don't seem to be taking this seriously.'

'Perhaps because it has nothing to do with me.' At last Laidlaw raised his eyes from the cards to stare at Meade. 'I'm sorry because it is obviously important to you. It's probably extremely important to Dugdale as well. But like I say, I'm not responsible. And really don't expect me to shed tears over a man who not only fought against the South but massacred some of its boys and then for no reason whatsoever, because after all, he came out of it all with money and health, raised his sons to continue to hate the South.'

'Like you said, the War has been over a long time.'

'Pity Dugdale didn't realize the same. Listen, I'd never heard of the Dugdales until I arrived in Sycamore Corner and got into a poker game with Gordon. He said some harsh things about me and the South. Which I didn't appreciate. But not so that I'd shoot him from ambush. If I'd been inclined to do so I would have done it there and then.'

Exactly what everyone said.

'Why did you leave town the next day?' Meade asked. 'Were you frightened of what might happen?'

Laidlaw laughed. 'Not frightened, no. I'm a gambler — I can handle myself. But I saw enough violence in the War to last me a lifetime and these days I spend all my time as a peace-loving man avoiding trouble.'

'Gordon did threaten you.'

'Yes, but I didn't take his threats particularly seriously. He was drunk and angry. But it just seemed the sensible thing to do to come on here where I hoped he and his family wouldn't find me and string me up just for being from the South. I stayed because I soon learnt that the Dugdales weren't likely to head this way and I was also told that Gordon was a bit of a blowhard and that once he'd sobered up he wouldn't go running to his pa about a Rebel being in town.'

Meade wasn't so sure about that.

'I'd have left real soon if I found out different. I'm afraid you've had a wasted journey.' Laidlaw sighed. 'You'll just have to take my word for it when I say I'm innocent or waste more of your time in asking everyone in town about what I've been doing since I arrived.'

And Meade thought that *would* be a waste of his time. Laidlaw could have killed Gordon but not shot at Louis nor caused the fire in the kitchen without being away from Leeville for several hours during which someone would have missed him. He was also a pretty good judge of character and he couldn't see Laidlaw as a cold blooded murderer. All the same he decided to ask Marshal Freeman to keep an eye on the man in case he was wrong.

A word of warning wouldn't go amiss to Laidlaw either.

'Don't go anywhere else just yet,' he said, finishing his beer and standing up. 'And be sure to stay in Leeville and don't venture anywhere near the Broken Spur. Dugdale's ready to shoot anyone he thinks is guilty.'

'Very well, sir, I'll be sure to do as you tell me. I wish you luck so I can be on my way when I do want to leave.'

20

Although it meant a longer ride Meade decided to return to the Broken Spur before going on into Sycamore Corner. He needed to tell Dugdale what he'd found out, so the rancher didn't try to find the Southerner for himself and dish out his own punishment, and he also wanted to make sure everything was still all right there. On the way he pondered about who could be guilty.

Ralph Addington — no. Piers Laidlaw — extremely unlikely.

Someone at the ranch? As far as he knew the only newcomer was young Tommy Walker and surely either Dugdale or Hoskins would have mentioned anyone else who had recently been employed. As for Tommy, he didn't seem likely and he certainly didn't have a southern accent, but, well, he hadn't been there long and he was in the hills all alone when both Gordon and Louis were shot with no one to see where he was or what he was doing. They only had his word for it that Louis hadn't reached the meadow where the cattle were. Tommy could have shot him there and then moved the body. Meade didn't really believe that but it was a possibility and he decided to keep an eye on the young man.

Otherwise it could be a man who had been at the ranch for some time before putting his plans into action. He'd have to ask Hoskins for the names of anyone employed in the last year. Or was the killer hiding out nearby, a man none of them knew, the horseman Katie Bowen had seen riding away?

After checking in with Hoskins, who said everything was under control, he went on up to the house and found Dugdale sitting alone in his study. The man was obviously drinking steadily for the bottle of whiskey on the desk was almost empty, but all the same he didn't appear the worse for wear.

Meade thought it would take him a long time to drink enough to blot out what had happened and the knowledge that it was his fault. Certainly Meade wouldn't like to be in his shoes, not now and not when he had to confess everything to Celia.

'I've been wondering what to do,' he said in a slightly slurred voice. 'Stay or go? Run away or fight?'

'How can you fight when you don't know who your enemy is?' Meade sat down opposite him and stretched out his legs.

Dugdale didn't look pleased at that but he wasn't stupid. Despite all his ranting and raving, his demands for something to be done, he knew how difficult finding the killer was proving, especially as it obviously wasn't Doc Addington. If only it had been. As it was, although he didn't like admitting it, it might well be one of the men he employed and trusted.

He slammed the glass down on the desk with such force that it cracked and broke, spilling whiskey over the papers. He took no notice, perhaps didn't even notice.

'So, Meade, what do you advise?'

'I'm not certain you, your family and especially Louis are safe out here. I can't protect you nor can Sam Cassidy.'

Dugdale's head slumped forward. 'You're right, goddamn it.'

'You must consider your family.'

'Yes, their safety is paramount.' The man sighed. 'Nothing else matters. Not the ranch. Not my position in society. Certainly not money.' He thought for a moment or two then made up his mind, feeling better when he had done so. 'I'll send Celia and Ella back to Maine for a while. I've still got several relatives there who'll gladly take them in. No damn Johnny Reb will be able to reach them all that way away.' With an abstracted air, he began to collect up the pieces of broken glass.

'No, I doubt the killer would be able to trace them that far or go after them if he could. But what about Louis? He can't travel all that way.'

'You think he'd be better off in town don't you?'

'Yes. It was different before but now the ranch is vulnerable to attack. You don't know who to trust. But Cassidy has people there he *can* trust to set up a guard on Louis and whose background he knows and who cannot possibly be guilty.'

'Very well.' Dugdale nodded.

'And you, sir, what will you do?' Meade rather hoped Dugdale would agree to return to Maine as well but he didn't think it likely, and he was right.

'By God, Meade, I'm not turning my back on this. I've never been a coward and I refuse to start being one now. I'll stay and face the bastard down. End this one way or the other, once and for all.'

★　★　★

Slowly Louis opened his eyes.

He lay in bed in his room. It was dark

because for some reason the curtains were drawn across the windows, although beyond them he could tell it was broad daylight. Something moved and he turned his head to see his mother sitting in a chair by his side.

'Mother.' His voice came out as a croak.

'Louis!' Immediately Celia was up and bending over him, wiping his face with a cool cloth. 'Are you really awake?' She rested a hand on his forehead. Thank God, still no sign of a fever. Surely, oh surely, that meant he would be all right, would recover.

'Some water.'

Celia poured out water from a carafe into a glass and held it to her son's lips. 'Just a sip, dearest. That's good. How do you feel? Oh, son, we've been so worried.' She wiped tears from her eyes looking at Louis as he lay back down. 'But you'll get better now. I'll fetch your father and Ella. They'll want to see you.' She turned away.

Beyond the door Louis saw a young

cowboy sitting outside in the hallway, gun held ready in his lap. Before he could wonder why and before his mother could come back to him he drifted off into sleep again.

★　★　★

'I won't go!' Ella was adamant.

Dugdale looked at Meade who smiled slightly in sympathy. After going to see his son the rancher had called his family into the study and told his wife and daughter what he planned for them. Ella was proving difficult. She was too much his daughter to want to run away.

'We've always been safe on the ranch,' she continued. 'We will be now. We'll be safe with you and Dick Hoskins to look after us.'

'Ella, listen, I want your mother away from here and you must go with her to protect her. I can't think about how to find and stop whoever is doing this to us while I'm worrying about you two.

And stopping him is of the greatest importance right now so we can go back to being a family again. You must see that.'

'Mother?'

Celia put her hands out towards her daughter. 'I want nothing more than to leave the Broken Spur, Arizona and the West and enjoy some peace and quiet in Maine. But,' she bit her lip, 'Gus, dearest, I really don't want to go without you or Louis.'

'I won't leave you, Dad.' Ella went up to him and put her arms round his neck. 'Please don't make me. You shouldn't be on your own.'

'Gus, please come with us,' Celia begged. 'Please.'

'No,' Dugdale said firmly, putting Ella away from him. 'I will not be forced out of my own home. Besides how can I expect others, such as Meade and Cassidy, to take risks for me if I'm not willing to take them for myself. My place is here, helping to find this killer and bring him to justice.'

'Ella's right, you can't stay here alone,' Celia said.

'I won't be alone. Hoskins will be with me. And I'd trust him with my life. I shall be all right.' Dugdale caught hold of his wife's hands. 'And I shall feel better once you and Ella are safe from harm. Sending you to Maine is the best way to protect you both. And Meade here has said he'll help escort you to the railhead. Put you on the first train East.'

'Why can't you do that?'

'Because I have the ranch to run and I've been neglecting that side of things for too long.'

Meade realized there was something else behind Dugdale's decision to remain behind on his own and so did Celia if her apprehensive look was anything to go by. But the man was adamant over what he was going to do and neither of them could change his mind.

'It means I have to leave Louis behind. I won't know how he is. And he can't be moved to town yet. It'll be too long a journey and too hot.'

'We'll travel early tomorrow morning before sun's up. He'll be comfortable enough in the buckboard. Please, Celia, don't prove difficult.'

Mother and daughter looked at one another. Neither was happy, neither wanted to leave Dugdale and Louis, but they both knew that when Dugdale got that look on his face and used that tone of voice there was no arguing with him. They would have to do as he said.

'I'll ask Mrs Bowen and Katie to help you both pack a few things for the journey and to prepare early breakfast tomorrow.'

'All right, dear,' Celia with a little sigh. 'I just hope the both of you know what you're doing. Mr Meade, I hold you responsible for ensuring my husband's safety. And for coming back here as soon as you've delivered me and Ella to the train station.'

Meade nodded.

'It'll soon be over,' Dugdale told her.

'Then I'll send for you to come home.'

Saying no more Celia went upstairs to sit by her son and to say goodbye to him. She wondered if once she left she would ever see him, Gus or the Broken Spur ever again.

21

Cassidy spent an anxious afternoon wondering how Jeremiah Meade was getting on. He felt sure Meade could take care of himself but there was always the chance he could be shot from ambush just as the Dugdale boys had been. He hoped not. Besides liking Jeremiah, it wouldn't look good if a man from the governor's office was shot to death near Sycamore Corner.

In the end, knowing it was no use worrying over something beyond his control he went down to the saloon for a drink and talk with Tony Vaughan. He'd been neglecting his town duties for the last few days and Vaughan would be able to tell him what was going on.

And it was there that Meade found him.

'Let's sit down.' Cassidy signalled to Vaughan for a beer for the other man.

'There's a table free in the corner where we won't be disturbed. How's things?'

'First off, I doubt very much whether Laidlaw is guilty. I don't see how he can be. He says he's been in Leeville for nearly all the time since leaving here and quite a few people there are willing to back him up. Which means I'm right and the killer is most likely employed at the ranch.'

'Makes sense to me,' Cassidy said with a nod.

Meade took several gulps of his beer. 'Dugdale agrees and so there's been a change of plans. He's sending his wife and daughter back East to Maine. They're leaving tomorrow.'

'Good idea.'

'I think so. I'm not sure Celia and Ella feel the same. But it'll be a weight off my mind to know they're on the train and out of harm's reach. I said I'd go to the railhead with them and a couple of the cowboys. I'm not expecting any trouble on the way but is there anyone in town who'd come with us? Another gun would be handy and be a deterrent.'

'I'll see what I can do. Who's going with you from the ranch?'

'Hoskins' right hand man, chap called Pete Simms.'

'Yeah, I know him. He seems reliable enough.'

'And I asked for Tommy Walker to come as well.'

Cassidy raised his eyebrows. 'I thought you suspected him.'

'I do. Well sort of. Enough to want him driving the buggy where I can keep an eye on him, not setting up an ambush somewhere along the way or at the ranch settling scores with Dugdale. Sam, will you do something else for me?'

'Sure, what?'

'Find out the times of the trains east. I don't want to reach the railhead just to see the train steaming away nor do I want to have to wait there too long.'

'Yeah, I can do that. I think there's a

couple call each day. Iffen they don't have the information at the stage office I'll send off a telegram to the railroad office in Tucson. And, Jeremiah, don't worry too much about the journey. Once you get beyond the sycamore grove and out into the open you should be OK. It's quite flat and empty that way. No one can ride up on you and there ain't any places where you can be dry-gulched. Should only take about an hour.'

'Good.'

'Isn't Dugdale going with his women-folk? I'd've thought he would.'

'No, he's staying at the ranch with Hoskins close by.' Meade frowned. 'I'm not too happy about that. I've the feeling that Dugdale is trying to draw the killer out so he can attack him in some sort of final showdown. And he wants me out of the way while he does so in case I try to stop him.'

'That would be typical of the man,' Cassidy agreed. 'In a way you can't blame him.'

'No, I suppose not. And in the end it might be the only way to prove who the killer is.' All the same Meade had a bad feeling about it all. 'I just hope Dugdale doesn't do anything stupid or find he's bitten off more'n he can chew. It might not work out like he's planning.' And then he would have a dead rancher to explain to the governor.

'What's happening about Louis?'

'He's being brought into town so that he can stay with Ralph. On my way here I called on Ralph and told him. He was quite pleased because he's still worried about his patient and doesn't particularly want to be riding back and forth to the Broken Spur to care for him. He's going to get a room ready. Sam, can you arrange for men to protect the doctor's house? And arrange a rota so the place is never unguarded at any time.'

'Sure. Have to pay 'em though.'

'The governor's office will meet the bill.' Meade waited until Vaughan came over with two more beers before going on. 'By the way did you get any answers to those telegraphs I asked you to send?'

'Yeah. Here you are.' Cassidy pulled a couple of crumpled pieces of paper from his trousers' pocket and handed them to the other man.

The governor's staff had been efficient as usual. The information included the date of the court-martial, the name of the accused, as well as the officers for the prosecution and defence, those sitting in judgment and the names of the witnesses. Lieutenant Dennis Shipton was the only one speaking for the prosecution while Sergeant Drake was one of several for the defence, although what defence there could be Meade didn't know. Then came the names of the seven Confederate soldiers and their ages. He sighed. They were no more than boys. The youngest was sixteen and the oldest only twenty. He scanned their names. At the bottom of the paper was the verdict: Not Guilty. How could that be justified? Except that war excused a great deal and a civil war seemed to excuse more than most.

Meade tapped the paper. 'Do any of these names mean anything to you?'

'No.'

'I'll give them to Dugdale, see if he recognizes any of them.' Although he doubted whether the killer, if he was a relative of one of these boys, would be using his own name.

The other message concerned Lieutenant Shipton. Quickly Meade read it. There wasn't much information on the man.

'It seems he left the army as soon as the war was over and nothing more has been heard of him.'

'So he could be the one I guess.' Cassidy was doubtful.

'Maybe. Not likely though. It'd take a powerful motive for someone to seek revenge after all these years and being bawled out by your commanding officer isn't probable.' Meade looked at his companion. 'What's up, Sam, you look like you've got something on your mind.'

Cassidy paused for a moment, wondering whether to say anything or not, thinking Meade might consider him foolish. Then he said, 'Jeremiah, you know there's a whole lot about this situation I don't understand.' Meade nodded. 'But in particular something happened at the ranch, roundabout the time of the fire, something was said, that's got me real puzzled.'

'What is it?'

'That's the trouble I can't remember. I've been trying to work it out since Ralph and I got back to town.'

'Perhaps if you don't think about it for a while it'll come back to you.' Meade smiled. 'That usually works for me. We'll talk it over when I get back.'

'Yeah, OK. Now I've got things to attend to. I don't want Louis shot at again, especially while he's here in town.' He stood up. 'I'll see you in the morning before you set out.'

'Sure.' Meade watched him go. He was glad he had someone like Sam Cassidy on his side, because he was

243

proving his worth as a lawman and as a friend. He leant back in his chair. He was worried about the next day, wondering if it really was the right thing to do. He knew he could rely on Sam but had he done everything he could and should to protect the Dugdales? He knew he wouldn't be able to relax until Celia and Ella were on the train and were safe.

'Hi, honey.'

He looked up and smiled as he saw Christine standing by his side.

'You look like you could do with some company.'

'You're right. Sit down. I'll get us some beer.' He signalled to Vaughan. 'How are you?'

'I'm lonesome too.'

'Really?'

'And cross that you ain't been to see me since you've been here.' Christine reached across and stroked his arm.

'I'm sorry. I've been busy.'

'Are you busy tonight?'

'No.'

'Then perhaps we can be company for one another?' She gazed longingly into his eyes.

'You're too young for me, sweetheart.' Meade almost smiled at the way she pouted at him. 'But you can stay and talk for a while, can't you? Tony won't mind.'

'I'd like that.'

22

It was early the following morning when the Dugdales arrived in Sycamore Corner. Meade and Cassidy and the townsmen recruited to help guard Louis waited for them at Ralph Addington's house. And alerted by gossip and talk that something big was going on plenty of people were out on the streets as well.

As well as several cowboys from the ranch, Dugdale and Hoskins rode next to a buggy driven by Tommy Walker, with Celia and Ella in the back, neither looking particularly happy. Bringing up the rear was a buckboard with Louis lying on its bed, slipping in and out of sleep.

'Any trouble?' Meade asked going up to the rancher.

'None.' The man dismounted and flung the horse's reins at Hoskins who caught them expertly. He went over to the buggy to help his wife and daughter down. 'I agreed Celia could wait here until Louis was settled.'

Meade nodded. 'That's OK. The train doesn't leave until 11 o'clock. We've got plenty of time.'

'Do you want any more of my men to go with you to the railhead?'

'No. Tony Vaughan is coming as well. I think it's more important that you háve plenty of men with you at the ranch. I'm sure that's where the danger lies. I really can't see the killer following us.'

'Fair enough. Be careful there!' Dugdale swung round as Louis was being lifted out of the buckboard.

Ralph took a quick look at his patient and smiled, seeming satisfied by what he saw. 'Take him into the bedroom,' he said and led the way into the house to show the men the way.

Celia went with him while Ella stood as close to her father as possible without actually touching him.

Dugdale turned to Cassidy. 'You have men ready to guard Louis?'

'Yes, sir. Both outside and inside the house, day and night. Everything is in hand.'

'I'm worried the bastard might try to attack him again.'

'Don't worry. We all know we've got to keep our eyes peeled.'

'Good, thank you.'

Meade hid a smile thinking that it must have taken quite an effort for Dugdale to thank the town marshal, of whom he had been so scathing.

'I'll just go and see that Louis is all right. Ella, come with me.'

'I'll be glad to get on my way,' Meade said to Cassidy.

'Won't be long now.'

And indeed it was shortly afterwards that Dugdale came out of the doctor's house, a weeping Celia by his side, and Ella talking with Ralph.

'Time to go,' Dugdale said as they reached the other two men. 'Don't fret, my dear,' he added patting his wife's shoulder, 'you know this is for the best.' He shook Meade's hand. 'Look after them for me.'

'You know I will. I'll come out to the ranch as soon as I've put them on the train to let you know they're safe. And, sir, you be careful too.'

Dugdale nodded grimly.

From the look in the man's eyes Meade was sure he intended to resolve this without recourse to the law, even though it meant taking chances and risking his life.

'You will be all right on your own, won't you?' Celia wiped her eyes with a tear-stained handkerchief.

'Of course I will. I looked after myself in the army, didn't I? Came out without a scratch.'

'That was a long time ago.'

'Don't you worry about me.'

But everyone knew that both Celia and Ella would worry all the time, especially as they were going so far away.

'Come on, let's be off.' Meade

mounted his horse. He wanted to be away from Sycamore Corner.

Dugdale kissed his wife and daughter goodbye and helped them into the buggy. They set out with Pete Simms riding in front and Meade and Vaughan bringing up the rear. They all carried their rifles out and ready.

Cassidy went with them to see them safely through the sycamore grove, which he thought was the only likely place that an ambush could take place. Once they were through the grove and out into the open on the other side he left them to continue on their way while he decided to call on Ralph, make sure the arrangements he'd made were in place and then . . .

What was that? A noise from somewhere amongst the trees. He pulled his horse to a stop and looked round, hand going automatically to his gun. Another movement. A fleeting shadow. Then what he realized must be a Rebel yell! With heart-stopping clarity he knew it wasn't Meade and the others who were in danger of being ambushed, it was him!

Cassidy didn't bother with pulling the rifle from its scabbard. Instead he flung himself off his horse just as another rifle barked and he felt the bullet whine by his ear. He fell awkwardly and heard the crack of a rib breaking, causing him to cry out. Another shot and the next bullet struck him in the side. God, whoever his attacker was he was a good shot! Screwing his eyes up against a sudden jolt of pain he somehow managed to retain a hold on the horse's reins and the frightened animal was suddenly between him and the killer.

Even so several more shots followed but while they all came close they missed him and the horse. By now Cassidy had clawed his pistol out and coming up in a crouch he fired back, although he had no clear target and his hand was shaking too much for him to hit anything anyway.

There was another yell, followed by

the sound of a horse galloping away. Then no more.

Trembling with reaction Cassidy got slowly to his feet. Breathing hard, he leant against his horse and peered into the trees. Nothing and no one. The danger was over.

'There, there, boy, it's OK,' he whispered stroking the horse's neck. 'We're safe.'

It was then he realized that he was in a good deal of pain and he remembered he'd been shot and cracked a rib. He looked down. His shirt was sticky with blood and carefully he pulled it aside to see a deep and ugly hole gouged out along his side. It was still bleeding. He hoped it wasn't a bad wound because he really couldn't be incapacitated now. He wasn't worried about his broken rib. That could be bound up and would soon mend. But a bullet wound could lay him low for quite a while. Hell!

With a groan he pulled himself up into the saddle and clung there for a minute or two as the trees seemed to whirl round him.

He decided to ride out of the sycamore grove and back on to the streets of the town as quickly as possible, just in case he was wrong about being safe and the ambusher was still around. He just hoped he'd make it.

*   *   *

Meade was pleased that Cassidy was right when he said the way to the rail-head was flat and open. There was no possibility anyone could follow them without being seen. Nowhere to lie in wait.

'What happens when we get back?' Vaughan asked Meade as they rode along. 'What are you going to do?'

'I'll go out to the Broken Spur, start asking questions there.'

'Perhaps now the killer knows you're on to him he'll give up and leave. He might think he's punished Dugdale enough by killing his eldest son and disrupting his whole way of life, making him feel vulnerable for probably the first time ever and forever wondering if the danger is over or not.'

'Maybe.' Meade wasn't convinced.

And he didn't think that Dugdale would be pleased if that did happen. Dugdale wanted his own revenge. As for Meade, he wanted to know the killer's identity and bring him to justice because whatever reason he thought he had for what he'd done there was no excuse for killing an innocent young man any more than there was an excuse for what Dugdale had done in Georgia.

'Well, Louis should be safe enough at Doc's and,' Vaughan looked round, 'we'll soon have Mrs Dugdale and Ella on the train and they'll be out of harm's way too.'

'A good thing too.'

They spoke too soon. For it was only a little later that the accident happened.

★ ★ ★

'You'll live,' Ralph said as he bandaged Cassidy up. 'The bullet wasn't very deep and the wound isn't infected. As for the rib it'll hurt like hell and I advise you not to do anything too strenuous for a while but it's a clean break and won't present any problems.'

'Thanks.' Cassidy went to get up.

'No.' Ralph pushed him back down. 'You lie still. You might not be badly hurt but you have been shot. And you've had a shock. Drink this.'

'What is it?'

'Something to help you sleep for a while.'

'But I can't. I've got things to do.'

'Yes, you can. Doctor's orders. Don't worry. Both you and Louis are under guard here. Go on, drink it. Good.' Ralph turned away to wipe his hands on a bloody cloth. 'I wonder why the killer targeted you.'

'Me too.' Then Cassidy knew. 'It must be because he somehow realized, perhaps from my face or attitude, that I suspected something was wrong. He was scared I'd be able to work out what it was and when I did I'd know his identity.'

And the thing was he had and he did!

All of a sudden he remembered what had puzzled him, what hadn't made sense at the time, but made perfect sense now.

Should he get someone to ride after Jeremiah, tell him? But the Dugdale party wasn't being followed because the killer had ridden away in the opposite direction.

Dugdale then? He should be warned. He was riding back into danger.

'Who is it?' Ralph asked coming back to the bed. 'Do you know?'

'Yeah,' Cassidy's voice was slurred and as he started to tell Ralph what he'd figured out the medicine worked and before he could stop himself he fell into a deep sleep.

23

Thankfully they weren't travelling fast when the accident happened. It would have been much worse if they had.

The buggy hit a rock half hidden in the grass and bounced down on the ground with a thump hard enough that Celia and Ella were jerked almost off their seats. Not that there was anything unusual in that when travelling in Arizona but this time one of the wheels began to come off, sending the buggy tipping to one side.

'Hell!' Meade said and both he and Vaughan called out a warning.

It was too late. Realizing something was wrong the horses took it into their heads to break into a startled gallop. Tommy Walker did his best to stop them, pulling hard on the reins, even as they got away from him. In the back Celia and Ella clung to one another,

Ella screaming wildly.

'Quick!' Meade yelled and spurred his mount into a gallop.

Vaughan was close behind while Simms came from the other direction.

The horses didn't get far. Almost as soon as they started their run the wheel span away. The buggy began a slow roll-over, slowing the animals too. Tommy was flung from his seat to land in a heap among the horses' hoofs. The two women were trapped, helpless, as the vehicle crashed down on to the ground, tipped on one side, and was pulled a short distance until Simms reached the horses. Somehow he dragged them to a scared, sweating halt.

'See to the animals,' Meade shouted at him. 'Make sure they're all right.'

He and Vaughan dismounted, running over to the buggy. His heart was beating fast as he wondered what they would find.

Thank God, Tommy was alive, was already sitting up. He was white-faced with shock and pain, holding his left arm that hung down by his side. Ignoring his cry of pain Meade quickly pulled him away from the thrashing hoofs of the horses and away from danger.

'Don't move,' he ordered rather unnecessarily. 'Mrs Dugdale,' he added urgently, 'Ella.'

They were already emerging out from under the wreckage of the buggy. To his immense relief neither looked too badly hurt. Celia had a cut on her forehead which was bleeding heavily while Ella's hands were grazed and her jacket had a long rip in it. It could, he knew, have been a lot, lot worse.

'Are you all right?'

'I think so,' Celia said in a dazed voice.

'Stay still, both of you, for a moment or two, get your breath back.'

'What happened?' Ella asked.

Meade hunkered down in front of her. 'Don't cry. It's over. You and your mother are both safe. Mrs Dugdale, have you a handkerchief or something

259

you can hold to that cut, try to stop it bleeding?'

'Yes.' The woman pulled a handkerchief from her jacket pocket and with a shaky hand held it to her forehead. It was quickly covered with blood. 'Was it an accident?'

An accident!

Accidents did happen but Meade thought one was unlikely in the circumstances. It was much more likely to have been a deliberate attempt at sabotage in order to hurt or kill. It would have been easy enough for the buggy wheel to be loosened and he doubted very much if anyone had thought to inspect the vehicle before they started out that morning. He certainly hadn't done so. Then it would be a sure-fire bet that somewhere on the journey, going over rocky and uneven ground, the wheel would come off. As it had.

He shuddered to think what might have happened had the horses been going faster or if they had been travelling down a slope; as it was it was lucky that the three occupants of the vehicle were all more or less all right.

'Or was the wheel tampered with?' Celia continued, thinking along the same lines as Meade. 'Has someone tried to kill us like they did poor Gordy?'

'There's no way of knowing. But if so they haven't succeeded.'

'No. Come here, dearest.' Ella was still crying with shock and Celia caught her daughter in her arms and held her close. Looking over the girl's shoulder she noticed Tommy Walker still sitting on the ground. 'What's wrong with him?'

'I think his arm is broken.'

'Poor lad. None of this is his fault. It's not fair. Please, Mr Meade, find out how he is.'

Meade left the Dugdales in the care of Tony Vaughan and went over to Tommy. 'How do you feel, lad?'

'Sick,' Tommy mumbled.

'What about the horses?' Meade

looked at Simms.

'They've calmed down. Shall I cut 'em loose? I don't think we can use the buggy.'

'Do that.' Meade didn't see how they could do so either. One side was smashed in. They had nothing with which to repair it. They were in the middle of nowhere.

Hell!

He went over to the wheel, studying it. And was joined by Vaughan.

'Was it deliberate?'

'I can't tell. But it's a bit of a coincidence isn't it?' Meade didn't like coincidences.

'Sure is. Jeremiah, what are we going to do?'

'We'll have to go back to town.'

'Dugdale won't like that.'

'What choice is there? Mrs Dugdale needs that cut seen to. It's bleeding badly and might even need stitches. She and Ella have had a shock and Tommy's arm will have to be set and put in a splint. With no vehicle they'll have to ride. And I don't think any one of them is up to riding far. Sycamore Corner is nearer than the railhead.' Thank God they hadn't gone a great distance. 'I doubt there's a doctor at the railhead whereas Ralph Addington is in town.'

'Yeah, you're right. What about the killer? Is he out there somewhere watching?'

'No. This was done in the hope of causing the mayhem it has and perhaps if he'd been lucky some real damage. I still believe the killer is waiting for Dugdale at the ranch.'

Vaughan nodded.

'At least I know Tommy Walker isn't responsible. He'd hardly risk getting hurt himself.'

'That's right.'

'We'd better get started. Ladies.' Meade walked back to Celia and Ella who were now on their feet by the wrecked buggy their arms around each other. 'We'll have to return to Sycamore Corner.' He was a little amused to see that neither seemed upset about that.

Celia asked, 'How we will get there?'

'Mrs Dugdale, you and Ella can ride my mare and Vaughan's horse. We'll ride the buggy animals. Will you be able to do that?' he asked the saloon-keeper, who nodded. 'And Simms can take Tommy up behind him. Your bags can be tied to the horses' saddles. It won't take us long. We haven't come far. Once there we'll go straight to Ralph's so he can doctor you all.'

Celia nodded. 'Come along, Ella.' She took hold of her daughter's hand and marched her over to the horses. 'You've been raised on the frontier to be an independent young woman, capable and brave. A buggy accident in which thankfully none of us is badly hurt shouldn't worry you.'

Even so Meade wasn't surprised to find that as he helped the woman up into the saddle she was trembling despite her brave words.

As they rode out he was certain it had been no accident and he was afraid the killer now had them exactly where he wanted them: heading back to Sycamore Corner and the Broken Spur ranch.

* * *

A decision was made. Plans changed. It was becoming too dangerous to delay any longer. A pity. But if possible Dugdale's family could still be finished off and then the hated Dugdale name would be lost forever and good riddance to it. If it wasn't possible it didn't matter all that much. The most important thing was that it was the right time for Dugdale, the bastard, to face up to his crimes.

Time for him to die!

24

As they reached the Broken Spur, Dugdale turned to Hoskins. 'Go and see to the horses, Dick, and make sure the men are alert and ready for trouble.'

'Will you be OK on your own?'

'Yes.'

With heavy footsteps Dugdale went into the house and along to his study. He sat down at his desk, too worn out even to pour himself a whiskey. He'd thought he wanted to be alone but now that he was he found the place deathly quiet and stifling. He put his head in his hands for a moment. He missed his family already, oh so much. What would he do without Celia? For years she had been by his side, supporting him, loving him, and now not only was she and his darling little Ella not with him but Gordy was dead and Louis shot and wounded.

At least Celia and Ella must be on the train East by now, well away from any danger. And surely Louis was safe in town. He'd better be or Cassidy and Addington would answer for it.

He groaned. None of this was their fault, it was his, and it was no use taking it out on them.

But it would be over soon for he was certain the killer was nearby, would attack him before long. He would be ready.

He roused himself when there was a knock on the door. 'Come in.'

It was Maybelle Bowen. 'You're back, sir. Did Mrs Dugdale and Miss Ella get away all right?'

'I think so. I hope so.'

'Me too, sir. And how are you?'

'Not all that good.'

'Well, sir, don't you fret none. Me and Katie are here to look after you. While I get your supper ready how about a nice hot mug of coffee and a sandwich? That'll perk you up.'

Resisting the urge to tell the woman

not to fuss, Dugdale nodded. 'Thank you, Mrs Bowen, I'd like that. And, Mrs Bowen,' he called after her as she started out of the room, 'thank you and Katie for staying. You didn't have to you know.'

'Oh but, sir, we wanted to. Very much.'

* * *

As the cavalcade of horses came to a halt outside the doctor's house, Ralph ran out, a look of consternation on his face. 'Jeremiah, what the hell has happened?' he demanded.

'There was an accident. Mrs Dugdale and Ella have been hurt and Tommy's arm is broken.' Meade jumped from the horse and went to help Celia down while Ralph hurried up to Ella. Over his shoulder he said, 'Simms, take the horses to the stable and, Tony, can you stay around just in case. Let Sam know — '

'Sam's inside,' Ralph interrupted.

'He's been shot.'

'What!'

'Don't worry, he's not badly hurt. He's sleeping now and should be OK when he wakes up. He also cracked a rib. Mrs Dugdale, Miss Ella, come on inside, so I can tend you.'

'What about my son?' Celia asked, leaning on Ralph as he helped her up the path.

'He's peaceful. You can see him as soon as I've tended to that cut.'

It was a while later that Ralph came to find Meade, who was sitting in the kitchen, drinking coffee with Vaughan.

'Nothing to worry about,' he said. 'Now I've washed it, Mrs Dugdale's cut isn't as bad as it looks and doesn't need stitches. Ella's hands are grazed and painful and she's got some nasty bruises on her arms but that's all and I've set Tommy's arm which luckily was a clean break.'

'Can they go back to the Broken Spur yet?'

Ralph shook his head. 'I wouldn't

recommend it. They've been shook up. Best leave it until tomorrow at least. Anyway, I thought you thought the killer was at the ranch?'

'I do. I'd better arrange for a room at the hotel for the Dugdales. Make sure they're well guarded.'

'That won't be a problem,' Vaughan said. 'Townsfolk might not like Dugdale all that much but they ain't got any quarrel with Mrs Dugdale and Miss Ella. And young Tommy can stay at the saloon if Doc ain't got room for him.' He looked at Ralph who shook his head.

'I've got two patients' beds and they're both occupied.'

'I doubt whether anyone is after him anyway.'

'OK, thanks. Simms can stay in town to help while I ride out to the ranch, tell Dugdale what's happened. Find out what he wants to do next.'

'Wait a minute.' Ralph caught at Meade's arm. 'You ought to wait until Sam wakes up.'

'Why?' Meade wanted to get on his way.

'Before he went to sleep the last thing he said was that he knew the killer's identity.'

So then all that was left to do was wait.

And fret. And wonder.

★   ★   ★

It was late evening and Meade was at the café eating thick slices of beef and mashed potatoes and drinking coffee when Ralph came to find him, to tell him that Sam was awake.

'He's a bit groggy,' he added as they set out for the surgery. 'But he's remembered what he wanted to tell you.'

'Thank God for that!'

Cassidy was sitting up in bed. His face was white except for dark shadows under his eyes but he managed a smile as Meade came in.

'You all right?' Meade asked, pulling

up a chair to sit by him. He motioned for Ralph to stay.

'Felt better. Could've been worse.'

'You sure it was the killer shot you?' A lawman made a great number of enemies during his line of work.

'Yeah. I heard what I took to be a Rebel yell. It was that what saved me actually. I was already dropping out of the saddle when the shooting started.' Cassidy plucked at the blanket. 'Jeremiah, I was shot because the killer realized I'd thought something strange had happened at the ranch and was worried I might put two and two together and come up with the answer.'

Meade sat forward. 'And now you have? You've remembered what it was? You know who the killer is?' He was aware of Ralph coming slightly closer, as eager as he to learn what Cassidy had to say.

'Yeah.' Cassidy closed his eyes for a moment against a spasm of pain. 'Katie Bowen said she saw a man riding away from the ranch, didn't she?'

'That's why I went to see if I could find any tracks.'

'Earlier, she said.'

'Yes.' Meade began to get an inkling of what Cassidy was talking about and a prickling started up and down his spine.

'But, Jeremiah, that doesn't make sense. Presumably this rider was meant to be the killer who set the range on fire. Someone so clever he managed to sneak into the house with no sign of a break-in and despite the cowboys patrolling around outside.'

'He was already inside,' Ralph said. 'Like Dugdale said. Like he accused me.'

Meade waved a hand for Cassidy to go on.

'Ralph's right because otherwise he must have broken in when it was too dark to be spotted, right? After which he got out of the house, again without being seen, and then waited nearby to make sure he'd been successful in setting the fire. But that's not what

Katie said. According to her she saw the rider *before* the fire started. Riding away. So why wait around at all? If he wasn't going to make sure there was a fire why not ride away at once before anyone but the guards were awake and when it was still dark. Why wait until people were up and about and he might be spotted and so risk being chased and caught or shot? Don't forget we're talking about someone who up till then had been too clever even to be seen let alone caught. Now he takes a risk like that for no reason whatsoever.'

'You're right,' Meade agreed. 'It doesn't make sense. Unless — '

'Unless the Bowens were the ones who set the fire!'

'Why would they risk being hurt when the range blew up?' Ralph said, sounding very shocked. 'And Katie was hurt, don't forget.'

'Not badly,' Cassidy pointed out. 'And don't you remember how Maybelle turned on me when I said so. It wouldn't've been that big a danger.

They could've kept out of the way, shielded themselves somehow. Then pretended that Maybelle had to drag her daughter out of the kitchen. That way they not only tried to set the ranch house alight but cleverly deflected all possible suspicion away from themselves, made it appear as if they were in as much danger as the Dugdale family.'

Meade sat back, a stunned look on his face. Cassidy was right. The Bowens, mother and daughter, had to be the killers. It was the only thing that made sense. God!

He was furious with himself. He should have worked it out earlier. Instead he'd hardly taken any notice of what Katie had said beyond presuming that the rider might be the man he was after, which was clearly the intention. He'd been so eager to follow him, and catch him, that he hadn't thought things through. He shook his head. He even knew the Bowens hadn't been at the ranch very long yet he'd not once considered them.

How could he have been so blind? Had he been fooled by the Bowens simply because they were women and it didn't seem possible that women could be guilty of so much hate? Or had they spent so long planning and plotting they were able to fool everyone? Katie's remark was the first mistake they'd made.

Because if it had not been for that and were it not for Sam Cassidy realizing something was wrong, they might never have been suspected at all. Until too late.

'What I can't figure is why?' Cassidy said. 'What has turned two women into killers?'

Meade thought about that for a moment or two. 'How old would Maybelle Bowen have been in 1864? She's in her early thirties now. So she'd have been seventeen, eighteen then. And Katie is sixteen. Supposing one of the seven dead Confederates was Maybelle's husband and she was pregnant with Katie when he was killed

276

in The Atrocity.'

'There wasn't a Bowen amongst the names of the dead men,' Cassidy said.

'A name can be changed.'

'But two women,' Ralph said. 'To do all those terrible things. It's so cold-blooded. And Katie is so young — ' He broke off.

'I reckon Maybelle must have always wanted revenge on Dugdale and so she raised her daughter to feel the same. It's a sad situation all round. I could almost feel sorry for them. Except of course for the fact that they are killers who don't seem to spare a thought for their victims.'

'Or the likes of Mrs Dugdale who wasn't responsible for The Atrocity but is suffering because of it,' Cassidy added.

'And now Dugdale is alone with them in the house. He won't suspect them either.' Meade got to his feet. 'I'll ride there now and hope I'm in time.'

But he feared that Dugdale could even be dead already. Knowing that

Sam Cassidy was still alive, and it had been another mistake not to finish him off, he had a feeling that the Bowens would fear they would soon be found out and so would be anxious to be on their way, go somewhere they could change their names again and not be caught. He couldn't let that happen.

'I'll come with you,' Ralph offered.

'No, you won't. I want you to find Tony Vaughan and send him after me. I can't waste any time.'

'Good luck,' Cassidy said. 'I wish I could go as well.'

'I'll be OK.'

As Meade was shrugging into his coat and about to leave the house, Ralph came up to him. 'Jeremiah, I've just looked in on Louis. He's awake. He wants a word with you. Says it's important. Have you got time?'

'Yes, all right.'

Louis lay propped up against several pillows, looking much better, even with a little colour in his cheeks.

'Mr Meade,' he said in a croaky

voice. 'I've remembered something about that Rebel yell. It was made by a woman. A young woman too.'

Katie Bowen!

25

'Time for the bastard, Gus Dugdale, to die,' Maybelle said to her daughter.

Katie smiled, a nasty unamused smile, quite unlike her usual pretty one.

They both held Colt .45s in their hands as they approached the study.

'Let me do the talking.' Maybelle's carefully trained voice slipped back into her Georgian drawl. That would shock Dugdale rigid! Almost as much as when he learned that she and Katie were responsible for all that had befallen him. His oft-stated declaration that he never employed Southerners and never would was about to be shot to pieces just before he was shot to pieces as well.

'OK, Ma, don't make it too quick though.'

'I've no intention of that.'

'Let him suffer.'

Without knocking, Maybelle and Katie entered the study where Dugdale was doing his best to deal with some paperwork. He glanced up, an annoyed look on his face at the sudden interruption, before his eyes widened in shock as he saw the two women both pointing guns at him.

'What the hell?' he exclaimed, rising to his feet.

'Sit down,' Maybelle ordered. 'And put your hands on the desk where we can see 'em. Don't try anything silly or we may have to kill you sooner than we planned. Before you learn the truth of what you did to me and mine and that would be a shame, wouldn't it? Oh, but don't worry you're going to die soon enough.'

Katie giggled and turned to shut and lock the door.

'As you may have noticed, my daughter and me are from Georgia, the hated South. That's right, sir, we're Southerners!'

'What is the meaning of this?'

Dugdale demanded angrily, nevertheless doing as he was told.

'Oh la di da,' Maybelle mocked. 'Hark, Katie, the master in his study making demands of his servants. He wants to know what we mean when I would've thought it only too obvious.'

Of course Dugdale didn't have to be told. He knew. He was furious with himself. He had never once suspected the Bowens. Had shut himself up in the house alone with them. Thought the threat would come from outside. Had taken no precautions.

'You killed Gordy and shot Louis,' he accused Maybelle.

'Not exactly,' she said with a little shake of her head. 'Actually it was Katie who shot your sons. She's a much better shot than I am — '

'She still didn't kill Louis.'

'Only because his horse was startled.' Katie gave a sulky pout. 'Got him three times though. He should've died and would've if Meade hadn't interfered. Should've shot him too.'

'You might still get your chance, dear,' Maybelle told her. 'But we've got other more important things to deal with first. And Mr Dugdale, I've decided that I'm to have the pleasure of shooting you.'

'But why?' Dugdale's hands were clenched on the top of his desk.

'Why?' Maybelle screamed. She stepped forward, pointing the Colt directly in his face.

Katie laughed as he winced and drew back.

'You dare ask me that. When you've got the list of the boys you slaughtered somewhere on your desk. Oh, let me tell you all about them.' Tears came into the woman's eyes but she blinked them away. 'They were just boys, you know that, don't you? They were exhausted. No threat to you or General Sherman. It was near the end of the War. You could've let 'em go on their way. They were in no state to do anyone any harm but, no, you had to shoot 'em down like dogs.'

'They were the enemy.'

'Don't you dare try to justify yourself to me! They were just scared, tired boys and you must know that in your heart. One of 'em was Karl Webster. He'd just turned eighteen. Had his birthday two weeks before. And he and I were betrothed. We were going to be married as soon as the fighting was done. We grew up in a small hamlet, being born just a few days apart, and I'd loved him all my life and he had me too. We meant everything to each other.'

This time the tears ran unchecked down Maybelle's cheeks.

'It's all right, Ma,' Katie said trying to comfort her.

'Then we heard he was dead.' She laughed, a bitter harsh sound. 'Oh, that was bad enough but at first we thought he'd died for the cause we all believed in. Then, oh Mr Dugdale, then, we found out how he'd died. Shot down while he was surrendering.'

'Along with six others,' Katie put in.

'An incident I think you call it. But

an incident so bad you were court-martialled for it.'

'I was found innocent.'

'Innocent!' Maybelle laughed again. 'You were never innocent, you were as guilty as hell! And those who judged you were no better'n you. We couldn't go after them but we could go after you. It's taken a long time but here we are. And you know something, I'm glad you got away with your crimes because now you know what it's like losing someone you love and you'll go to your grave knowing that me and Katie are still around and wondering if we'll ride into town when we're done here and finish off the rest of your damn family. Which we will.'

'You bitch!' Dugdale half rose from his seat but had no choice but to sink back down as the women raised their guns.

'Ella is the bitch and an arrogant one at that,' Katie said with a sneer. 'She thinks she's so much better than me but she won't feel quite so important when she's grovelling at my feet begging me not to kill her. Just before I pull the trigger.'

Dugdale had no doubt that the girl would carry out her threat. 'You leave my daughter alone! Do you hear? Or — '

'Or what?'

Maybelle smiled. 'Best of all, I get to kill you myself rather than see you shot in front of a firing squad.'

'Shoot him, Ma,' Katie urged.

Maybelle silenced her with a lift of her hand. There was more to tell. 'It was a short time after Karl's murder I found I was pregnant. My family threw me out and at seventeen I was left alone to cope with the loss of my beloved Karl, with having a baby and then raising her. Have you any idea how hard that was? How hard life was in the defeated South. What I had to do to survive? No, of course you haven't. You've always led a privileged life.' She indicated the room with a wave of her hand. 'It was when my little Katie was born, right there and then, when I had no idea how I was going to cope or how my daughter and I would even have enough money to live on, that I decided we would find you and make you pay even if it took the rest of our lives.'

'So you brought up your daughter to hate me as well?'

'Isn't that what you've done with your family? They hate the South because of you for which there was no real reason as the War was good to you,' Katie said.

'Oh, Mr Dugdale, what laughs me and Katie have had watching you and your darling wife go to pieces over the death of that stupid idiot you called your son.' Maybelle paused. 'It was a shame about Louis. He wasn't like the rest of you but he was your son and so he had to be punished too.'

'You won't get away with this.'

'I don't see why not.'

'I won't let you.'

Maybelle looked at Katie and laughed. 'You're in no position to do anything either to help your family or to stop us.

You might think you are. You might think you can draw your gun before I pull the trigger or maybe you hope I won't have the guts to pull it at all. You'd be wrong on both counts.'

'And if Ma don't I will.'

'Think about this as you're dying, Mr Dugdale, Katie and me will disappear into the night and come morning all that will be left behind are dead Dugdales!'

And Maybelle raised her gun and fired.

★ ★ ★

The shot sounded just as Meade was pulling the tired mare to a halt in front of the house. He leapt out of the saddle and raced for the door, drawing his gun as he did so. Surely, he couldn't have got there just seconds too late.

★ ★ ★

At the same time Dugdale roared and stood up, tipping his desk over with a resounding crash. The bullet aimed for his heart gashed his arm instead as, taken by surprise, Maybelle jumped backwards. Katie screamed in anguish and fired as well. But although Dugdale was hit he was already rolling to one side, drawing his own gun.

★   ★   ★

Meade gave the door a hefty kick. The lock shattered. He burst into the room.

'Hold it right there!' he yelled.

'Nooo!' Maybelle screamed. 'No!'

She swung towards him and shot several times, wild shots that hit the walls and furniture and ricocheted round the room.

Meade was left with no choice. He aimed and fired. At exactly the same moment Dugdale fired from where he lay on the floor.

Both bullets struck Maybelle Bowen, spinning her round and down. She had time to cry out just once before she fell on the carpet. And didn't move again.

'Ma! Ma!' Katie cried. 'You bastard!'

Before she could fire the gun she carried Meade flung himself at her, grabbing at her arms and hands, forcing her to drop the Colt. Held tightly, she still managed to kick and claw and punch. She was like a wildcat and it was with some difficulty that he retained his hold on her.

Over her shoulder he saw Dugdale scramble unsteadily to his feet. The man approached Maybelle and quickly kicked the gun away from her hand, although it was obvious she was dead. Then he kicked her several times before looking towards Katie, a darkness in his eyes.

'Put your gun down,' Meade ordered. 'There'll be no more killing here.'

'She shot my boys,' Dugdale snarled. 'It was her.'

'I said put the gun down. She'll stand trial for murder. She's unarmed. I will not have her shot in front of me.'

To Meade's immense relief, because he didn't know what he would have done otherwise, Dugdale lowered his gun. Perhaps he too thought there had been too much killing. Just at that moment Hoskins came running in. He was, thank God, followed almost at once by Tony Vaughan.

'Sir, what's up? We heard shots. My God!'

Meade felt Katie go limp in his arms. She burst into wild wailing and knowing she had given up and presented no more threat he let her go to Maybelle. She fell on the carpet beside her mother, crying and cursing.

'You're hurt, sir,' Hoskins said going up to his boss.

'Not badly. I'll live.'

'Unlike Gordy,' Katie sneered. 'You'll have to live with your loss for the rest of your life.'

'Be quiet,' Meade said, still fearing she would be shot out of hand.

'It was the Bowens?' Hoskins was hardly able to believe it.

Dugdale slumped into his chair and rubbed his face. 'They were going to kill me too. Oh for God's sake get her' — he indicated Maybelle — 'out of here. The other one too. Lock her up somewhere until the morning when we can take her into town.'

'Yes, sir.'

Meade pulled Vaughan to one side. 'Tony, go with them, make sure no harm comes to Katie.'

The saloon-keeper nodded.

'I'll kill you yet,' Katie screeched as Hoskins went to lead her away. 'While there's a breath left in my body I'll come after you. You'll never be safe. Neither you nor your damned family. Remember that.'

'Shut up,' Hoskins told her and none too gently dragged her away, Vaughan following on close behind.

'Don't worry,' Meade turned to Dugdale. 'She won't have the chance to do you any more harm. Even if she doesn't hang she'll be locked up in prison for a very long time. Probably never get out.'

Dugdale shook his head. 'I don't

know. All the while she's alive there'll always be a risk.' Then he smiled slightly. 'No, perhaps you're right, Meade, perhaps she won't have the chance.'

26

'I'm off soon,' Meade told Cassidy a couple of days later.

The marshal was recovered from being shot and thankful to be up and about again, although his rib was still giving him a jolt or two.

'So I'll say farewell and thanks for all your help.'

He had already been to see Ralph Addington and Tony Vaughan to thank them as well and said goodbye to Christine, who said she would be heartbroken to see him go; although naturally he didn't believe her. Word was also going to be sent to Piers Laidlaw that he was in the clear and could be on his way.

The morning before, Katie Bowen had been up before a magistrate and arraigned for trial for murder and attempted murder. The trial would be held at Tucson where she was going to be moved as soon as the necessary arrangements for taking her there could be made.

'That can't come soon enough for me,' Cassidy said. 'I'm a town marshal used to dealing with cowboys who've had too much to drink and tax evaders, not cold-blooded murderers. I want her out of my town.'

'She won't give you any trouble.'

Both men looked towards the girl in the jail cell. She lay on the bunk, arm across her face, a picture of abject misery.

'She's seen her mother shot dead and most of their plans for revenge have failed because Dugdale is still alive and so is his family apart from Gordon.' Meade shook his head. 'All those long years of hating and waiting and planning. All wasted. I know what Dugdale did was wrong but it was just as wrong of Maybelle to bring her daughter up to hate him so much that she wanted nothing in life other than to kill him.'

'It's beyond me,' Cassidy admitted.

'I'm not making light of her loss but if only she could have found the strength to put it all behind her she and her daughter could have had a good life together. Instead,' Meade shrugged, 'in her last moments Maybelle must have known she was leaving Katie to face the hangman.'

* * *

Except she didn't.

It was a couple of weeks later when the newspaper headline read: 'Killing at Tucson Jail.'

Meade's heart sank.

And the report stated: 'Late last night Miss Katie Bowen who with her mother, Maybelle, wreaked havoc on Gus Dugdale, one of the Territory's richest and most famous ranchers, and his family, and who was awaiting trial for the murder of Gordon Dugdale, was found shot dead in her jail cell. At the moment there is no information as to how it happened or who was responsible. The sheriff is making inquiries but . . . '

Meade put down the paper. He knew who was responsible. Gus Dugdale. Oh not personally but he had hired someone to kill the girl and that person had gotten to her inside jail where she should have been safe. Who knew how? Perhaps a jailor had been bribed, perhaps someone had gotten himself arrested especially to be near Katie. It didn't matter. And the reason why was obvious. Dugdale wanted to take his own personal revenge for what she and her mother had done and because he didn't want to take the chance that somehow, sometime Katie would still come after him and his family.

Meade knew he wouldn't be able to prove it. But he wished he could.

Because while Katie deserved to hang that was for a judge and jury to decide, not Dugdale. It wasn't right for the rancher to take the law in his own hands, especially when all that had happened was partly his fault.

Sighing, Meade stood up. He went outside. He wanted a breath of fresh air and a drink. Take the taste out of his mouth.

THE END